SECOND CHANCES

True Tales of Heartbreak
and Reconciliation

On Newsstands Now:

TRUE STORY
and
TRUE CONFESSIONS
Magazines

True Story and *True Confessions* are the world's largest and best-selling women's romance magazines. They offer true-to-life stories to which women can relate.

Since 1919, the iconic *True Story* has been an extraordinary publication. The magazine gets its inspiration from the hearts and minds of women, and touches on those things in life that a woman holds close to her heart, like love, loss, family and friendship.

True Confessions, a cherished classic first published in 1922, looks into women's souls and reveals their deepest secrets.

To subscribe, please visit our website:
www.TrueRenditionsLLC.com or call **(212) 922-9244**

To find the TRUES at your local store, please visit:
www.WheresMyMagazine.com

SECOND CHANCES

True Tales of Heartbreak
and Reconciliation

From the Editors
Of *True Story* And
True Confessions

Published by True Renditions, LLC

True Renditions, LLC
105 E. 34th Street, Suite 141
New York, NY 10016

ISBN: 978-1-938877-59-9

Visit us on the web at www.truerenditionsllc.com.

Contents

RISKED IT ALL FOR—COMFORT FROM A STRANGER

I leaned over the edge of the bridge and looked into the water. I was trying to peer beneath the surface of what would end my miserable life once and for all. It had taken me nearly an hour to walk to the water and I needed courage, for I was a coward of the worst kind—afraid to live and afraid to die. I was trapped in an abyss of misery that pulled me down deeper each day.

A low, distant rumble roused me from my reverie. I watched a motorcycle as it sped across the highway that led to the bridge. As it neared the driver slowed, so I faced the water again, not daring to make eye contact with the stranger who seemed to be watching me with an intense curiosity.

I continued to look away even as the driver pulled over to the side of the road. When he got off of his bike, I turned to watch as he pulled his helmet off. His dark hair spilled across his shoulders in a haphazard tangle, his black boots were as worn as his faded jeans, and his gray T-shirt had streaks of dirt and dust from the road. I made no move to run or even walk away. Like a deer caught in headlights, I was powerless. But it wasn't fear that held me in my place. It was apathy. If he were there to rob and kill me, so be it.

Perhaps the choice of life or death is no longer mine, I thought.

Part of me hoped that was so. Part of me wanted this stranger to take away my choice and put me out of my misery.

"Hey," he said, walking closer.

Instinctively, I took a step backward. The cool, metal rail of the bridge pressed against my back.

"Are you all right?"

I wrapped my arms protectively across my chest. "Yes, I'm fine," I answered quickly, wondering where this encounter would lead.

"Oh, okay," he said. "When I saw you standing there. . . ."

"Yes?" I asked.

"I'm sorry. I'll leave you be, but it's not every day that you see someone standing on this bridge at five-thirty a.m. I thought maybe you had a problem."

With those words, it was as if something inside of me broke.

1

I simply didn't care anymore. "I won't have a problem once I convince myself to climb up on this railing and take a flying leap!" I blurted out.

"You don't want to do that," he said softly.

"Do you think I'm standing here for my health?" I asked sarcastically.

"I don't know what to say except that I'm pretty certain that the longer you stand out here the worse it'll be for your health."

I shrugged and looked out over the water. Dawn was beginning to break and the sky had taken on the slightest tinge of pink. The streets remained silent and it was still dark enough to jump without drawing attention to myself. This motorcycle gang member would be the only witness to the end of my very unremarkable life.

"It really doesn't matter. It's not your problem. But thanks for stopping by."

"Oh, great!" he growled.

"What's wrong with you?" I snapped. How dare he intrude on my misery!

"I can't walk away and leave you here."

"Why not?"

"Because I can't. Is there someone I can contact for you? A friend or a relative?"

"If I had a friend do you think I'd be here right now?" I asked.

He shrugged. "You might. Depends on how good a friend you had."

"Well, I have news for you, mister—"

"Mike."

"Mr. Mike?" I asked with a snort of laughter.

"Mike Leary. You were saying?"

"I have no friends. I have no family. At least not here."

"Where are they?"

"On the East Coast. My family, that is. I have no friends back east or here."

He rubbed his hand over the whiskers on his chin and watched me for a moment, sizing me up. "Can I take you to breakfast?"

"Why would you want to do that?" I asked.

"Why not? It's not like you have anything else planned, right?"

"True," I admitted in spite of myself. "But I'm not too keen on riding on the back of a motorcycle with a strange man."

"The only one here intent on harming you is you," he said. Then he turned and began walking to his bike. "Come on, take a break; you can kill yourself tomorrow."

"Do you have an extra helmet?"

His deep laughter belied his slim features. "A helmet? You must be kidding."

I settled onto the back of his bike and put my arms gingerly around his waist. "Yeah, hilarious. Sorry, but I'm not crazy about the idea of having my skull cracked on the street if you wreck this thing."

He set his black helmet on my head and fastened the strap. "The lady who wants to kill herself is demanding a helmet to protect her head. That's a good one." He laughed as he leaned on one foot to start the bike.

"I'm not demanding anything," I yelled over the roar of the engine. "I'd just prefer to choose my own method of dying."

He shook his head. "Some things are not for us to know. There's only one way into this world, but hundreds of ways out. Believe me, you're better off not knowing."

We sped through the empty streets. I had no idea where we were headed, but when I climbed onto the back of his bike, it was with relief. In my mind—my apparently very depressed mind—going with this stranger took the decision of life and death out of my hands and put it squarely into his. At the time, that convoluted way of thinking seemed normal to me.

The strong wind in my face invigorated me, giving me a sense of freedom that I hadn't felt in years. After only ten minutes, he pulled into the parking lot of a twenty-four-hour diner and turned the bike off. "I'm starving, how about you?" he asked.

"Not really," I admitted as I followed him. I nodded in thanks when he held the door open for me.

We settled into a booth overlooking the parking lot and ordered coffee and toast from a sleepy waitress. "Are you sure you won't have something else?" he asked.

"No, thanks. I don't have much appetite."

"Would you like to talk about why you were on the bridge?" he asked quietly.

"I'd really rather not, if it's all the same to you," I said.

"No problem. I'm not here to make things worse."

"I don't think you could," I admitted.

"The way I see it, as long as there's even a slim chance that things will get better, you should do all that you can to live and work through your problems."

"That sounds like a good idea," I answered. However, I hadn't the slightest inclination to take the stranger's well-intentioned advice.

He shrugged. "I do what I can. So," he said, changing the subject, "how long have you been out west?"

3

"Only about a month or so. I'm still living in a cheap motel. I suppose now that I'm going to live for a while longer, I'd better find myself a job or I'll be on the street."

"What sort of work do you do?"

"I worked as a secretary before my children were born. Then after my eldest came along, I quit work. I couldn't bear to leave my babies," I said, choking on my last words.

Mike reached across the table and put his hand over mine. "Then don't," he said quietly.

I cried quietly into my napkin. Unable to answer or continue my story, I merely nodded.

"I'm sorry. I didn't mean to upset you," he said.

I wiped my eyes and took a sip of coffee. "That's all right. None of this is your fault or your problem."

"I know, but if you want to talk about this more, I'm willing to listen."

"Thank you," I answered.

We finished our meal in silence and I thanked him as we walked to the parking lot. "What's your address?" he asked. "I'll drop you off."

I numbly rattled off my motel address and offered directions.

"You're staying there alone?" he asked as we glided from our parking spot.

I hesitated. Admitting to a stranger that I lived alone in a cheap motel didn't seem like a good idea. However, considering the circumstances, I decided that telling the truth really wasn't a big deal. "Yeah," I said. "I've been alone since I moved here last month."

"Will you be all right? No more thoughts of killing yourself?" he asked when he stopped his motorcycle in front of the motel.

I shrugged. "Either way, it's not your problem, but thanks for coming along when you did. Honestly, I don't think I would've jumped. I'm not brave enough."

He was quiet for a moment, searching for something to say. "You know," he began, "it takes more courage to live than it does to die."

"I don't know about that. I never felt like more of a coward than I did on that bridge. I wanted to jump, but I couldn't. If I knew of an easier way," I said softly, "I'd do it."

"What about your children?"

"I honestly think they'd be better off without me. I'm really sorry I involved you in my problems," I said, fumbling for my keys.

He wrote down his address and phone number on a piece of paper and handed it to me. "If you need anything—anything at all—don't hesitate to stop by or call."

I took the paper, crumpled it up, and then stuffed it in the pocket of my jeans. "Thanks; maybe I'll stop by sometime," I said.

A few days later, after I'd pounded the pavement looking for job only to hear that I was "not employable" because I hadn't worked in ten years and had no references, I found myself on Mike's street. Since he was my only acquaintance in town, I thought maybe he could give me a lead on a job or even allow me to use his name as a reference. Of course, using him as a reference would mean asking him to lie. After all, the only thing he knew about me was that I'm the suicidal lady he saw on the bridge in the wee hours of the morning. However, there was no one else in town who I knew, so I decided to take a stroll past his house and hopefully catch him at home. If he were home, I'd see where the conversation led and maybe I'd ask him for help.

I became confused when I realized that the address he'd given me was for a homeless shelter. I stood on the sidewalk and double-checked the address. Sure enough, the address on the paper matched the one on the outside of the shelter. Next to the shelter was a church and on the other side was a medical clinic. Surely he didn't live in either of those places. He seemed so together, confident, brave, and smart—and yet he's homeless? At that point, I realized that there was little, if anything, he could do to help me find work, but I figured that I might as well pay him a visit, anyway.

I gingerly pulled the door open. Inside was a beehive of activity. A long line of people waited for lunch while volunteers and employees hustled back and forth preparing the food and clearing and wiping tables. A young girl who looked to be around high school age sat in the corner surrounded by giggling children and read from a thick book of nursery rhymes.

"Hi, I'm Eddie. Welcome to The Tenth Street Shelter. Is there something I can do for you?" an older man with a thick moustache asked.

"I'm Sara," I said, offering him my hand. "I'm looking for Mike Leary."

"He's around here somewhere. I just saw him," he answered, shaking my hand. "Come along; we'll find him."

I followed him through the noisy kitchen where several elderly women prepared huge hams, green beans, and chicken soup. A jazzy Sinatra tune blared from the portable radio on the table as the women laughed and joked while they cooked, seemingly oblivious to the vast amount of work required to feed so many people.

As we passed through the kitchen and into the storeroom,

Eddie called for Mike and we finally found him waist deep in boxes and cartons of groceries.

"Sara, it's nice to see you again. Is something wrong?" he asked.

"No, no, not at all. I . . . I'm just surprised to see you . . . here."

"Why? This is the address I gave you."

"Yes, I know. I mean. . . ." I took a deep breath and blurted out, "You're homeless?"

Mike smiled and shook his head. "No, I'm not. Well, not any longer."

A warm blush crept up my neck and onto my cheeks. "I'm sorry. I didn't mean to pry into your personal business."

"Hey, don't stress over it," he said, putting the matter aside with good humor. "And your memory is correct. I didn't mention I'd been homeless. I didn't think you needed to hear any more sad stories. Anyway, what brings you down here for a visit?"

"Oh, nothing really," I said, shrugging and sitting on an empty crate. "I was in this part of town and thought I'd stop by for a quick visit."

"Any luck finding a job?"

"No, not yet," I answered sadly, deciding that I couldn't possibly ask him to give me a reference, at least not until I knew him better.

He turned his back and began emptying a huge, cardboard container, putting box after box of dried potatoes, macaroni, canned vegetables, and fruit juice on the long, metal shelves in the storeroom. "How about some lunch?" he asked.

"Oh, thank you, but no thanks. I don't want to impose."

He picked up his clipboard, signed several papers, and then laid the paperwork on a shelf. "Impose?" he asked, spreading his arms. "Look at this place. I may not have much, but I have plenty of food."

It was the largest pantry I'd ever seen. "Yeah, you've got a lot of stuff in here. But still, this is for people who really need it. It wouldn't be right for me to eat their food."

"Sara, you're still living in that motel, right?"

"Yeah."

"And you're not working?"

"No, not yet."

"What's the last thing you had to eat?"

I shrugged. "Last night I had a hamburger."

"And this morning?"

"Nothing, I was in a hurry to find work."

"Then will you please join me for lunch?"

"Thank you," I said. "I appreciate what you're trying to do, but—"

"Wait," he said before I could finish. "I have an idea. How about you relax and accept my offer in the spirit in which it's intended? Lunch. Nothing more."

I nodded in agreement and Mike led me to the large dining area I passed through when I'd first arrived at the shelter. I found a plastic tray and stood in line. Soon my tray overflowed with spaghetti, bread, string beans, a hot mug of soup, and a cup of coffee. My hunger overshadowed my pride as we found a small, round table in the corner and I devoured my lunch.

"Tell me how you came to be here," I asked over coffee.

"How I became homeless or how I came to work here?"

"Both," I said, settling comfortably into my chair.

"Well, I became homeless as a teenager. About ten years ago, my father walked out on Mom and me."

"Where did he go?"

"He got tired of being married and tired of being a father, so he packed up one day and left. Mom had no way of supporting us. She had a hell of a time finding work, and eventually, we lost the house and ended up in a shelter."

"This shelter? They eventually gave you a job?"

"No, not here. We lived down south back then. The shelter we went to did more than put a roof over our heads. I wanted to drop out of high school to help support my mother, but a counselor at the shelter wouldn't hear of it. She insisted that I stay in school. She told me I'd help my mom more if I received my education. She seemed like a pretty bright lady, so I listened to her."

"Did your mother ever find work?"

"Yes, as a matter of fact, she went back to school and became a nurse," he said, grinning.

"Wow, you must be really proud of her."

"Oh, yeah, I am. She's a great lady."

"And what about you? Did you finish school?"

"Sure did. I graduated from high school and then went straight to college and got my degree in social work. Then I got a job here."

"Now that's impressive," I said. "What do you do here?"

"I'm pretty much responsible for the day to day administration of the place," he said, looking around. "But my main interest is counseling. I received my master's in psychology last year and that's my passion."

"I suppose you're in the right place then. I can't imagine any group of people who need counseling more than the homeless."

Mike shrugged. "Yes, I offer whatever help I can, though some people's problems go deeper than just being down on their luck. We get our share of drug abusers, alcoholics, and severely mentally ill people, too. Some of them have to be referred to a hospital or a psychiatric center."

"Maybe you'll let me help out? Since I'm going to eat here, I'd like to do my share of the work. I mean, I'm not qualified to counsel people, but I could stock shelves and perform some administrative work. That would free up more time for you."

"Oh, that can be arranged," he said with a smile. "We never run out of things to do around here and I'm tired of being stretched so thin. Thing is, we have a tight budget. Most of us here are volunteers, though I do have one full-time opening, if you're interested. Meals are included."

"I'd love it! I really need to find a job."

"Well, stay today and we'll see how you do. I don't usually hire people impulsively like this. Is it a deal?"

I shook his hand and smiled broadly. "Deal!" I exclaimed.

After lunch, I worked with the other members of the shelter. I peeled potatoes, scrubbed pots and pans, helped with inventory and paperwork, and then helped the ladies prepare tomato sauce, pasta, and salad for the evening crowd.

When Mike invited me back the next day, I eagerly accepted. Soon, one day turned into two, and then two days turned into a week, and I'd settled into a comfortable routine. I made friends, had a reason to get up each morning, and since the shelter provided all of my meals, I had one less thing to worry about. However, all of those good things didn't matter. It was too late for me. I still felt uncomfortable within myself. My life was upside down and I had no one—absolutely no one—to blame but myself.

One evening I sat alone in my room staring at the old-fashioned rotary phone on the bedside table. I thought of my family and wondered if they'd take me back. My husband and kids were just a phone call away. I looked at the clock. It was ten p.m. back east. The kids were no doubt sound asleep and Bob was probably watching television. I reached for the phone and quickly made the long-distance call. My heart pounded as I waited for what seemed like an eternity for the connection to go through. Finally, the phone rang. And rang. I glanced at the clock again. I couldn't imagine where they could be so late in the evening. Then the answering machine picked up. "There's no one here to take your call. . . ." Bob's voice boomed on the recording.

Tears dripped down my cheeks. He'd changed the message

from my voice to his. They'd already forgotten about me! Their lives were going on without me as if I were dead and gone, and considering what I'd done, they had every right.

I curled up on the bed and shut my eyes. Sleep didn't come easily that night, but then again it hadn't come easily in weeks. I might've dozed for a few moments, but soon my eyes popped open. I was gripped with an idea. It was a deadly thought.

I stumbled to the bathroom and flipped on the light. Quickly, I covered my burning eyes from the brightness and opened the medicine cabinet. Using one hand to shade my eyes, I searched and finally found exactly what I needed.

I fumbled with the razor until I managed to remove the blade. Then I dragged it over my finger, watching as a thin line of blood appeared. I swiped the finger across the front of my nightgown and pulled up my sleeve.

My problem wasn't the fault of the motel's housekeepers and I didn't want to leave a huge mess that they'd have to clean up, so I settled into the bottom of the bathtub and adjusted my nightgown over my legs to provide warmth. Then without further thought, I lifted my wrist and slashed the blade across my flesh. I didn't bleed much at first, so I squeezed my arm until the blood began dripping quickly. I should've cut it again, but frankly, the idea of cutting the same wound repulsed me. However, cutting the intact wrist did not, so I gritted my teeth and cut as deep as my fear would allow. I dropped the razor, leaned back, and took several deep breaths. Then I waited.

I'd just shut my eyes when the phone began ringing. I didn't dare answer it. As far as I was concerned, it was too late. I wouldn't turn back. Soon the ringing became annoying and incessant, stopping every so often and then starting again. I shut my eyes and tried to block out the sound. Eventually, the ringing became distant and faint, and finally, I heard nothing but the sound of my own breathing.

I must've passed out, because the next time I became aware of my surroundings, my face was warm from the late afternoon sun shining through the bathroom window and there was a fierce pounding on the door of my motel room.

"Sara! Sara, are you in there?"

It was Mike, and he sounded frantic. "Yes," I whispered. Blood covered the front of my nightgown and dripped off my fingertips, making me sticky and wet. When I saw how much blood there was, I panicked and tried to get up, but tiny flecks of light danced before my eyes, and I felt dizzy to the point of nausea. My fingertips were numb and my wrists ached so badly that I couldn't use my hands to hoist myself from the tub. "Help," I croaked through parched lips. "I'm here," I cried.

Mike continued to pound the door. Then I heard a loud crash and the sound of wood splintering. Then the bathroom door flung open with a bang. "Sara! Sara, what have you done?" he shouted.

He ran from the bathroom and I heard him on the phone. I couldn't make out his words because I was sleepy. I rested my head against the cool tile and faded in and out of consciousness. All I wanted to do was sleep.

When I woke up at the hospital, a nurse helped me into a clean gown and then a doctor sewed and bandaged my wrists. Later another doctor came to talk to me, but I refused to discuss my reasons for the suicide attempt. I lay curled up, huddled under my blankets, and tried to shut out the world. I couldn't bear to face what I'd done.

The next thing I remember is waking up in the hospital with Mike sitting by my side. "I'm sorry," I whispered.

"You don't need to apologize to me, Sara. I'm glad I found you in time."

"Me, too. I don't know what got into me."

"Well, whatever got into you has to be addressed. You can't go on like this."

"I was just so alone and frightened. I thought it would be best if I just disappeared."

"Why? Why do you feel this way? What is driving you to this?" he asked.

"I'm so ashamed."

"Listen to me, Sara. I'm not here to judge you. I'm here because you're my friend and I want to help you."

I turned my head and stared out the window. It was late. It must've been after midnight because the parking lot was empty and the highway that runs past the hospital had only a few cars buzzing by and not the usual, incessant hum of traffic. "It started so innocently," I began. "My husband, Bob, and I bought a computer, and not long afterward we installed the Internet. That's when my troubles began."

Mike reached for the pitcher on the table and poured me a cup of water.

"Thanks," I said, taking a small sip. "I only wanted to have a bit of fun. I never expected to fall in love. I—I never expected to lose everything."

"Tell me what happened, from the beginning," he urged softly.

"Well, shortly after we got the 'Net, I joined a chat group. Actually, I joined several chat groups. I met plenty of nice people, but I hit it off with one man in particular, Larry. We had so much in common that we began to talk almost every night. Within a few weeks, I fell in love with him."

"But what about your husband?"

I smiled weakly. "My husband," I said thoughtfully. "Yes, I love him, but I became so wrapped up in a fantasy world that I forgot the things that really matter. I only planned on meeting Larry and maybe having a short affair," I said, blushing. I was ashamed to admit that stuff, but he didn't seem shocked or offended so I continued. "I thought I was in love with him."

"Love?" he asked. "This love has certainly wreaked havoc on your life."

I sniffed and reached for a tissue. "Yeah, no kidding. I'd get up at all sorts of odd hours of the night to talk to him. I slept all day and could barely stay awake in the morning to see the kids off to school. At first, Bob teased me—he said the Internet was worthwhile because I certainly got enough use from it. But then as time went on, I knew that he was getting annoyed with me. He'd make comments about 'Internet addiction' and my 'Internet boyfriends.' I'd laugh him off, but he had no idea how close to the truth he really was."

I paused and sighed. "My story is so pathetic. I had everything a woman could want—a nice husband and two great children. Now look at me! I fell in love with a faceless man on the Internet," I said, holding up my bandaged wrists, "and it ruined my life."

"Faceless?" Mike said, raising his eyebrows. "You didn't exchange photos?"

"No, not for months. He said he wasn't good looking enough. He was shy and embarrassed, but I loved him, anyway. I thought I was in love with him, so I told myself that looks aren't important because what we had went deeper than flesh. We were connected. We shared a spiritual bond and I just had to have him. I had to be with him."

"It sounds like you were hit really hard by this love. You couldn't live without him?"

"Exactly. But perhaps that's the nature of infatuation," I answered sarcastically. "The desire to have and to possess. Then once you possess the thing you think you love, the magic is gone and you finally see the object of your desire clearly."

"Tell me about him," he urged.

"He was a con man. Or maybe he really was magic. How else can you explain the effect he had on me? He was good, sweet, kind, and gentle—the ideal man. I thought he was my soul mate, my love. He knew all the right things to say and I fell for every one of his lies."

"What was he like in person?"

11

"At first he was good, but it didn't take long for me to realize that he wasn't the man for me. He wasn't attentive, he didn't care, and he had other women. I left my husband, the only man I ever truly loved, and it was the biggest mistake I've ever made."

"How did your husband react to all of this? Did he throw you out of the house?"

"No, he got sullen and quiet. He told me that it's my life and I'm entitled to live it however I see fit. I knew that my kids would be safe, so I told him that I wanted to explore my options."

"And what did he say to that?"

"He said it was my choice, but that I shouldn't expect to be welcomed back if I walked out.

Then I went to meet Larry. I was with him for about two weeks before I found out that besides me, he was seeing two other women who he met on the Internet. To him it was a game. He said he liked me, but it was his right to see other women since we weren't exclusively committed."

Mike sighed. "That must've hurt."

"Yeah, it did, but I sure couldn't complain, especially not after everything I'd done to Bob. So I decided to stay here for a while, try to find work, and hopefully make a life for myself. But it hasn't been easy."

"What now?"

I shrugged. "I don't know."

"Surely you must want something. What would you like to do with your life? You're still a young woman and you have children. Do you want to go home to your family?"

I gazed out the darkened window again. "Yes, I miss them so badly. But I'm too ashamed. I don't think they'll take me back."

"Would you like me to talk to your husband and find out his feelings? Maybe something can be worked out between the two of you."

"Oh, I don't know. I hate to impose on you further, and besides, I'm taking up all of your time. Surely it's not your responsibility to help me."

He shrugged his shoulders. "No, it's not my responsibility, but it's what friends do for each other."

"I don't think I've ever had such a good friend," I admitted.

He laughed. "Well, you do now." He put his hand on my shoulder. "Listen, I can't make any promises, but I'm willing to help you with your family. However, you're going to have to talk to a psychiatrist about the suicide attempts. I'm not qualified to help you there; only a doctor can help you get back on the right track."

"The doctor has already told me that. One of them, I suppose he's a psychiatrist, met with me earlier today. He prescribed medication and I can't leave until I'm feeling better."

"That's understandable," he said, taking my hand. "Cooperate with the doctor so you can get well and get on with your life."

"I'll try, and thank you for everything."

"I'm going to go now, but before I do, let me have your husband's phone number. I'll get in touch with him in the morning and try to explain the situation. We'll see if anything can be done."

I hastily scribbled the number on a scrap of paper. "Thank you," I whispered as he left my room.

I lay awake for the rest of the night trying to sort through my troubles, and as dawn lit the sky I finally fell asleep somewhat at peace. At least I could take solace in having found a friend.

Later that afternoon Mike knocked softly on my door before entering. "I didn't wake you, did I?" he asked.

"No, I can't sleep the day away. I have a life I need to put back together. Have you spoken to Bob yet?" I asked apprehensively as I sat up and pulled my robe over my shoulders.

"As a matter of fact, I have. I called him early this morning. Luckily, I caught him before he left for work."

I threw my legs over the edge of the bed and leaned forward. "Well? What did he say?"

"Well, Sara, I have good news, mostly."

"Oh, just tell me and get it over with!"

"Now calm down. I said good news. Bob is willing to come here and meet with you."

"When? What did he say? Will he bring the children? Can I go home? Will he take me back?" I fired off one question after another, eager to hear everything all at once.

"He's willing to see you, but he feels very betrayed by what happened, and rightly so. He'll arrive the day after tomorrow. He didn't tell me whether or not he'd take you back and he didn't mention the children. As a matter of fact, he still harbors a lot of anger toward you."

My shoulders slumped. "Then he may never forgive me. I might never see my children again."

"Whether or not he forgives you is up to him. Either way, it's your right as a parent to see your children. And Sara, may I offer a bit of advice before your husband arrives?"

"Sure, what is it?" I asked, eager to accept his counsel.

"When he arrives, before you get into an argument or any serious discussion, apologize to him and ask for his forgiveness. After all, you're the one who left. You walked away from your marriage, and though he's willing to meet with you, reconciliation and forgiveness may be a long, difficult road for the both of you. Frankly, I'm amazed that he agreed to come here. He must love you very much, indeed."

"I don't know how I can ever thank you, Mike."

"You can thank me by keeping yourself healthy and alive and reuniting with your children. You may only have this one chance, Sara, and I hope you take full advantage of it."

Two days later, I paced my hospital room waiting for Bob. When he finally arrived, there was no finer sight for my weary eyes. When he walked into my room, I thought my heart would burst with emotion. My first instinct was to run up to him and throw my arms around his neck like I used to when we were dating. But that was many years ago and there was no going back to those simpler times, so I took a deep breath and decided to face my future with dignity.

"Sara." His deep, familiar voice filled the small room.

"You didn't bring the kids?" I asked.

"No, I didn't think it would be a good idea. Your mother agreed to watch them until we sort things out."

I sat on my narrow bed and adjusted the folds of my skirt. One of the nurses had suggested that I dress, comb my hair, and clean up for my meeting with Bob. She thought it would give me a psychological advantage and make me feel better about myself and less vulnerable. She was right; I felt pretty good considering my marriage was in tatters and I owed my husband a huge apology.

"I'm sorry. Can you ever forgive me?" I asked, my voice barely above a whisper.

He looked up at the ceiling, around the room, and then focused on the bandages wrapped around both of my wrists. "It looks to me like you've already paid a pretty stiff penalty for your mistake in judgment."

Tears streamed down my face. I wanted to ask him to hold me, but I didn't dare. I was terrified he'd reject me.

"Can I come home?" I asked tentatively, bracing myself for the word no.

"It's your home. The kids miss you something fierce. I tried to return your phone call last night. I wanted to talk to you and hear your voice. I've missed you, Sara."

I took a few tentative steps toward him. "So, it's all right if I come home?"

"I never threw you out. You walked out all by yourself. It was your choice to leave and it'll be your choice to come back."

"Thank you," I whispered. "I don't know how I can ever make this up to you."

Bob shifted uncomfortably. "I don't expect this to be easy,

Sara. Everyone wondered where you were. Your mother was sick with worry and I had to tell her the truth."

"What about the kids?" I asked.

"I decided to tell them that you were off visiting relatives. I lied to them, but I didn't see what good it would do to tell the truth. They're too small to understand and they just want their mom back at home where she belongs."

"I'm so sorry, Bob. I never meant to hurt anyone. I don't know what got into me."

"The same thing that gets into a lot of people, I suppose. Cheating on your spouse isn't exactly a new idea," he said sarcastically.

"I never thought it would happen to us. Can you forgive me?"

He shrugged. "I forgive you, but we have a lot to work out and I honestly don't know how we're going to get through it."

"Do you want a divorce?" I asked.

"Right now I'm not sure what I want, but I'm willing to try and work something out. I won't keep you from the kids."

"For what my promise is worth, I swear to you I'll never run away again," I said.

Bob nodded and then rested his arm across my shoulders. "Well, that's a start, I suppose."

A week later I returned home with Bob and reunited with my children. While the children were happy to have me home and we easily returned to our routine, it wasn't so easy for Bob and me. We attended marriage counseling and though it was somewhat helpful, trying to hold our marriage together through that very difficult time was one of the hardest things I've ever done.

I'm sad to say that what was left of our feelings for each other couldn't keep us together. After six months of counseling, we came to realize that we couldn't erase the past and we couldn't forget about it, either. Bob and I decided on a trial separation, and during that time we realized that an amicable divorce was far better than raising our children in a household devoid of love.

Though Bob ceded half of the house to me in the divorce settlement, I still needed to find gainful employment to help support my children. Bob and I agreed on joint custody of the kids.

Ultimately, I found my way back to The Tenth Street Shelter and took a job as a full-time administrative employee. Thanks to Mike's friendship, I managed to pull myself together and return to my life. It took a good bit of time, but eventually I put the past behind me and learned to live with my mistakes and look forward to the future.

THE END

PIECES OF THE PAST:
I went looking for antique treasures—and found my lost love!

I'm a twenty-nine-year-old single woman and up until a couple of days ago, I considered myself to be a happy person.

I have a good job at a bank as a customer service representative and a good income. I have a dreamy apartment in an historic, Victorian house in town that I decorated in the country and shabby chic styles that I love.

My parents are wonderful. They're retired now and live directly on the beach in South Carolina, where I visit them often. I'm also close to my sister and her family. I love my nieces and nephews.

No, I've never been married. I've had lots of boyfriends, but no husband. And I've been able to live with that nicely—until that Saturday when I went shopping for a lace tablecloth at my favorite antique shop.

What I found was not a tablecloth, but memorabilia that brought back my painful past and all of the heartache I endured when Gary, my one true love, married someone else.

I thought I was over Gary. After all, it had been more than ten years since our high school graduation. But when you're in love as much as Gary and I were in love, you stay in love forever—no matter what happens. And I guess if I'm honest with myself, I have to admit that I still loved Gary after all those years. Even though he broke my heart.

We were seniors at Westside High School when we first discovered that our three-year friendship had turned into love. We met in the ninth grade. Gary and I came from two different middle schools that merged into one high school. We had a couple of classes together that first year and I thought he was the cutest thing I'd ever seen. His kept his dark hair cropped close to his head, his chestnut eyes twinkled when he looked directly at me, and he had smooth, olive skin.

By the tenth grade, he'd asked me out a few times. By eleventh grade, we were known as a couple around campus. We walked to class together when we could, met in the hallway in between classes, ate lunch together, and hung out before and after school. We went to ballgames, movies, and parties. Sometimes on lazy Sunday afternoons we'd drive up the Loop Parkway, pull over at a majestic overlook, and sit on the grass taking in the view and each other.

We went to the prom together—the highlight of dating season at the end of each year—two years in a row. We were truly in love. We talked about getting married one day after we both graduated from college and the time was right.

But, as the old saying goes, plans are made to be broken.

As much as we were in love, Gary and I tried our best to stay "pure" till we were married. That sounds prudish and downright silly in these modern times, but we were both from tight, rather religious families which upheld high moral principles.

It wasn't easy to avoid sex, though, because the way we heard it around school, most couples were doing it. Gary and I did lots of passionate kissing and explored each other's bodies in his family's sedan after dark on our dates, but full-blown sexual intercourse we held back on.

"I want to make love to you so bad, Anabelle," Gary groaned in my ear one night as our passion reached a particularly high level. "I want you to be mine completely." He kissed me again deeply. His body was pulsing.

My body was tingling, too, and urging me to forget all of the preaching and teaching I'd received from my parents and church and abandon myself to Gary. After all, we were going to be married someday. What harm would it do to seal our love forever by giving ourselves to each other? Surely God could find no sin in that.

"Gary, I want you, too." My breath was rising so rapidly that I felt like my lungs would explode.

But then, before we took that final step, we paused briefly, looked into each other's eyes, and sighed.

"No. We should wait," Gary relented with great regret.

"Yes," I managed, nodding. "We should wait."

We watched ourselves rigorously after that. We were careful not to allow our passion to get so steamy again. I suppose we both realized that with only a tiny push we'd slip into being lovers. As wonderful as we knew that would be, it might place obstacles in our path that we wouldn't be able to handle. Like pregnancy, for one. There were a thousand unforeseen bumps in the road that we couldn't even imagine, but we were mature enough to know that they'd be there waiting to mar our future.

Gary and I were as much in love as ever, and maybe even more. But we respected each other above all else and we sensed that we'd better cool off our relationship a little.

I realized how wise this was when my older sister, Jenny, and my mom casually injected this idea into the conversation one day. They obviously sensed how involved Gary and I were getting and how close we were at such a tender age to slipping over the edge to an unknown future.

Mom started first. "Anabelle, I love Gary. We all do. He's a great guy. But think about it: You're seventeen years old. He's seventeen years old. You're seniors in high school and you have years and years of life ahead of you. You need to date some other boys before you settle down with Gary."

"Mom's right." Jenny jumped on the bandwagon. "I know you love Gary. Or at least you think you do. But how will you know for sure if you never give another guy a chance? I mean, maybe someday you and Gary will end up married, but that day's a long way off. You don't need to go from this house to Gary's house without living a little. Do you understand what Mom and I are trying to say to you?" Jenny asked sincerely.

"Yes, but what if I lose Gary to another girl?"

"You won't, Anabelle. If your love is as strong as you say it is and you're destined to be together, you'll end up together."

"And when you two get old enough and the time is right for you to be married, you'll be glad that you waited. It'll be easier," Mom added.

"After you see a little of the world and mingle with other people, you should really test the love you say you have for Gary," Jenny continued. "That way, you'll start your life together—if that's what you choose—with a firmer relationship."

"You and Gary will be more mature and know for sure that you're right for each other as life partners," Mom declared.

Someone from Gary's family must've given him the same spiel. I wondered if his mother were in cahoots with my mother, although they didn't know each other.

By mutual agreement, Gary and I agreed to date other people during our senior year in high school. We still talked to each other on the phone periodically and when we passed in the hall, we stopped and talked. My heart leapt every time I was close to Gary and I looked into his warm, dark eyes. How can forcing ourselves not to be together possibly be good for us? I wondered.

Still, we dated others. One guy here, one there; it was the same for Gary with girls. But no other guy even made an impression on me. Only Gary sent goose bumps up my body.

If we were at the same ballgame or party with dates, Gary would keep an eye on me to see how cozy my date and I were becoming. I'd do the same to him and we'd catch each other spying.

That is, until Gary started dating Amanda Benton. Amanda was considered one of the prettiest girls in school. She wore great clothes and was known around Westside High as the spoiled, wild child of a wealthy businessman. It seemed that when she set her mark on Gary and dug in, he bit big time.

The pledge of love he'd made to me was all but forgotten when he was whipsawed by Amanda's attentions. She had a reputation of sleeping with any guy she dated. I had no way of knowing if that was true or not, but I suspected that it was.

Gary was with Amanda at school how he'd been with me. They were everywhere together. It broke my heart to see her take my place and it made me jealous.

I started dating Nathan, a jock on the football team, just to make Gary jealous. I cared nothing for Nathan other than friendship and he was so wrapped up in sports that he wasn't that interested in me, either. But when Nathan and I were together and Gary and Amanda were around, I played it up—big.

If Gary was in love with someone else, well then I would be, too. And Gary seemed to notice when I was trying to make him jealous, but he didn't know it was make-believe.

My hunch was that although he was involved with Amanda, he still had feelings for me. And I definitely loved him as much as ever. I didn't see how I could stand much more of seeing him with her. She was forever hanging onto him and snuggling up to him. It made me sick. It made me furious. It made me cry when I was alone.

Gary and I were supposed to date other people, but he wasn't supposed to fall in love with someone else—especially not with Amanda Benton.

Mom and Jenny were wrong. I'd already lost him.

Then one day Gary came up to me in the hallway out of the clear blue. It was near the end of the school year, about two months before graduation. He bored into me with his beautiful eyes. "Anabelle, I need to talk to you. Can you meet me after school someplace? Say in the park across the street?"

"Yes, sure," I answered, puzzled.

Why is he being so sweet to me now after weeks of practically ignoring me? I wondered.

It didn't matter. He made me melt like ice cream on a sidewalk. I would've met him if he'd suggested that we meet in Iceland. I had a practice session after school with the debate team, but I'd skip it. Nothing in the world was more important to me then than Gary. Maybe he was going to tell me that he was breaking up with Amanda and we'd pick up where we left off!

If Mom and Jenny disapproved, too bad. I'd tried it their way and it was pure misery. Gary was the only one for me then and forever.

I could hardly wait till the end of the day. The weather was perfect and warm. Spring flowers were blooming, the grass was green, and birds were singing. I was in love and Gary and I were going to get back together!

He was leaning up against a huge, oak tree waiting for me. His taut, toned body reminded me a little of Tom Cruise, only sexier. Gary smiled slightly when he saw me approaching.

"Thanks for coming, Anabelle. I have something I need to say to you." He looked me straight in the eye and sighed.

I couldn't figure out if he was happy or sad or worried or fearful or anxious. He lowered his eyes and seemed to take a deep breath before he began again.

I then realized that the expression on his face was dread. He was dreading having to tell me something. My breath caught high in my throat. "What do you need to say to me?" I didn't want to hear it, but I knew that I had to.

"No matter what you think, Anabelle, I love you. I always have and I always will."

I let his words penetrate my mind. He does love me. This is going to be good, after all! I thought.

Gary surely could see the hope on my face. He shook his head as if he understood what I was thinking and indicated that I was wrong. "What I mean is," he continued, "I'm in a bad situation. Amanda's pregnant." He hurled the news at me like a grenade.

I didn't think what he was saying was true. I must've heard wrong, I thought.

"Amanda's pregnant?" I repeated. "With your baby?"

"Yes." He dragged on, heavily, never removing his eyes from mine, "I wanted to tell you myself before you heard it from someone else."

He reached for my hands to steady me and keep me from collapsing on the ground. He eased me down onto the grass, propped me under the tree, and settled down beside me. Still holding my hands, he watched the tears roll down my cheeks.

"It's supposed to be me having your baby." I choked. It was a stupid thing to say, but it was exactly what I was thinking.

"Oh, God! I wish it were you. This wasn't supposed to happen. I can't believe it's happening!" he roared. He then released my hands and wiped away the tears under my eyes.

"But if you love me, how . . . how could you make love to Amanda?" I hated saying her name. I hated her. "You were

20

supposed to wait for me. Till the time was right for us. We were saving ourselves for each other!" I was yelling by then.

He was quiet for a few minutes before he spoke again. The words sounded weak and guilty. "I know I've betrayed you and what we had. Our future's gone. It's my fault and I'm really sorry. You'll never know how sorry, Anabelle," he lamented.

Yes, I thought I will know how sorry. Not only was he ruining his life, he was ruining mine, too.

"I'm so, so sorry." His expression was pained like he was facing a guillotine. I crumbled into his arms and cried openly. I think at some point Gary wiped a tear from his own eye.

I'll never forget the shock as long as I live. One minute I was filled with joy and hope and the next I was dead and in my tomb.

Gary talked to me for more than an hour. I remember every word he said almost as if I recorded it on a disk in my head. After we'd decided to date other people to keep from getting too serious, he regretted it. He couldn't stand the thought of another guy kissing me or putting his hands on me.

How was Gary to know that I barely let another guy kiss me? I couldn't stand the thought of anyone else's lips touching mine.

When Gary started hanging out with Amanda, he did it to forget me. He was ready to leave his innocence behind. Ready to grow up. Live dangerously. He was ready to become a man and Amanda was the perfect female to initiate Gary into that rite of passage. For a while, he was mesmerized by the whole sex thing. Amanda had him spellbound, he said.

But then he began to think of me again and the love we once shared. He didn't feel that kind of love for Amanda and he was ready to break it off with her. But before he got the chance, she dropped the bomb on him that she was pregnant.

We left each other that afternoon with the knowledge that we'd always love each other but that we could never be together. Not in this lifetime.

It was all settled. His family worked it out with Amanda's. Gary and Amanda would marry as soon as school was out. Nobody would have to know that Amanda was pregnant. She wouldn't show till summer.

They had a big, church wedding and a country club reception. I wasn't invited, of course. Nor would I have gone if I had been. I read about it in the newspaper.

I kept up with their lives for a while by reading articles in the local Westside paper, through friends and acquaintances, and from rumors Mom and Jenny heard around town. Mom and Jenny did their best to help heal my broken heart. I never held it against them for influencing me to break it off with Gary.

If it's true that all things happen for a reason, then we weren't meant to be together. But how could there by anything right about the heartache I felt?

Amanda's family money and position afforded lots of opportunities for them after they got married—or so went the gossip. Gary and Amanda moved downstate where Gary attended the university.

They had a little girl. I suppose few people knew that Amanda was pregnant before they were married, not that it really mattered.

After Gary graduated from college, he went straight to work at Amanda's father's company as planned. Gary worked as some sort of engineer, I think.

As the years passed, my heart mended and I quit trying to keep up with Gary's life. I had my own life and it was good. Not perfect, but good.

I also went away to college. Not to the State University, but to a small college in South Carolina. I saw a little of the world and mingled as Jenny and Mom had wanted me to do.

I took a job in Atlanta after graduation and worked there for a number of years. I experienced life, I guess you could say. I traveled a good deal. I dated various men. I nearly married once or twice, but each time I broke it off. I just never felt in love like I'd been with Gary.

I enjoyed my work and made plenty of money to provide for myself. What did I really need with a husband and a marriage that I wasn't really committed to?

Then the bank I worked for in Atlanta bought a smaller bank in North Carolina. My supervisors wanted me to transfer to the branch in my hometown of Westside to oversee the Customer Service Department and that suited me just fine. I was ready to leave the big city for a less hectic life and I jumped at the chance to return to Westside.

Although Mom and Dad no longer lived there, it was only a few hours' drive to the coast to visit them. And Jenny and her family had never left Westside, so I had them to keep me company.

Jenny had fun helping me rummage around in antique shops for furnishings for my quaint, new apartment. We often browsed in Fabulous Finds, and that's where I was that Saturday, only without Jenny. I was looking for a lace tablecloth.

Fabulous Finds is my favorite shop on Westside's Main Street. It has an eclectic mix of antiques and, some might say, rubbish. It's a cross between treasures and junk.

The owner, Edie, whom I'd come to know pretty well, has a

good turnover of merchandise because she sells her goods below what other shops might try to get for the same kind of stuff. Local people in town are always bringing their discarded items to Fabulous Finds. Whatever Edie thinks will sell, she displays in the shop. The remaining items go in the dumpster unless the local rescue mission can use them.

That Saturday afternoon I walked into the shop and asked Edie about a tablecloth. She pointed toward a shelf in the rear of the shop. "Pardon the mess up front," she said. "A bunch of stuff was dropped off here a couple of days ago and I just haven't had a chance to go through it yet." She nodded her head toward a couple of boxes that were piled on several pieces of furniture near the front window.

"Oh, boy! May I take a look?" It thrilled me to think that I might be the first to pick through the box of goodies.

"Sure," Edie said. "'Anything you see that you want, we'll agree on a price."

I stepped closer to the boxes that sat atop a two-seater sofa. Also stacked on the sofa were several blankets and bedspreads, a couple of sets of sheets, a pair of drapes, and some pillow shams. They looked practically new. Perhaps they'd been washed a time or two, but not more than that. Often people who redecorate their homes bring their old furnishings to thrift shops or antique shops to get rid of them. There were other items flung about on a chair that had obviously gone with the two-seater sofa.

"Have you found anything interesting?" Edie asked from across the shop. She was finishing up placing an arrangement of cut glass vases on an ornate, walnut table.

"There are some nice linens, but I don't need any. I haven't looked in the boxes yet."

"The woman who sent the stuff said that she thought I could probably get a good price for some of the bric-a-brac like the figurines and candy dishes. She said she wanted the stuff out of her house and to send her a receipt for the tax deduction." Edie grabbed a dust cloth and wiped off a few knickknacks and some shelves as she made her way toward me.

I opened the flaps of the top box and peeped inside. There were indeed china figurines and bluebirds. A gilded-edged mint dish and a mish mash of other glassware also filled the box.

"The woman had a man with a truck deliver the furniture and boxes. I only talked to her on the phone," Edie said. She stopped at a table and polished the glass top. An anniversary clock and a basket of marble, lawn-bowling balls were displayed on the table. "She said to dump anything I can't use. Said she was getting rid of her past and starting a new life. I bet I know what that means!" Edie chuckled.

"That's how you furnish your shop, isn't it, Edie?" I lifted the other flap and peered in at what appeared to be papers, photographs, and certificates of some sort.

"Oh, yes. People die and their children sell off their belongings. Retires downsize. And there's always just plain, old-fashioned divorce!" Edie said. She picked up a brass music box that used to hold cigarettes and dusted it. A couple of musical notes sounded when she set it back down. "Divorce brings in some of the best merchandise." She stood beside me and looked over my shoulder into the box.

I reached in and pulled out some faded snapshots of a boy on a bicycle. There were a couple of old car magazines, some old comic books, and a few copies of the Westside High School newspaper from one of the years I was there, of all things. Then I fished out a diploma from Westside High. The bold, black lettering jumped out at me. GARY LIGHT was the name of the graduate.

My heart leapt. "What?"

"Huh?" Edie murmured.

I rumpled through more of the box's contents. There were some photos of Gary when he was in college, with, I guessed, college pals. There was also a photo of Gary with two guys, obviously on a fishing trip. Strangely, there seemed to be no photos of Gary's wife or family.

Near the bottom of the box lay his high school senior picture in a silver frame. The glass over the picture had been smashed in the center and it shattered outward. It seemed like it had been struck, hard with a sharp object.

Under the photograph lay an annual from Westside High School. It was from the year we graduated; it had to be Gary's. With trembling fingers I lifted the annual from the box as if it were a precious artifact. There, in gold letters engraved on the padded cover, was the name GARY LIGHT.

I gasped.

"Do you know that person?" Edie asked.

"Yes," is all I could manage to say.

At that moment a customer entered the shop and Edie walked off to help her. I opened the cover gingerly and thumbed through it. I remembered the very spot where I'd signed Gary's annual as if it had happened just a week before. It was on the bottom of the page where my picture appeared. I even remembered what I'd written on that day long ago when Gary had brought his annual to me and pushed it toward me.

"Anabelle, would you at least sign your name? I need something of you to take with me." His eyes were filled with warmth and sorrow.

I returned his stare with mutual love that couldn't be mistaken, but I had to be careful what I wrote. It couldn't be anything telling that could be meaningful to anyone other than Gary. I wrote simply, "I'll never forget you. Anabelle."

I returned the annual to Gary and he pulled it to his lips and kissed my signature. That was the last contact I had with him. It was the last time we'd spoken. Shortly afterward, we graduated and parted forever.

How fateful was that—finding Gary's annual and some of his belongings after all that time? Well, it was absolutely crazy!

Edie showed her customer to the lampshade finial collection she kept in a cabinet and then helped a couple of other customers who strolled into the shop before she came back to me.

"Edie, can you tell me who sent these things to you?" I asked anxiously.

"Well, I don't see why not. Do you really know the person these things belong to?"

"Yes. It's an old high school friend. I can't imagine these personal items were ever meant to be discarded," I said.

"I have a hunch that they belong to an ex-husband like I thought." Edie raised an eyebrow. "The woman I talked to on the phone's name was Amanda something. Oh, I can't remember exactly. I'll go check. I wrote down her address and phone number." Edie strode off to her desk.

Amanda Light, I thought.

For some reason Amanda boxed up Gary's things and sent them away. Was it on purpose or a mistake?

"The woman's name is Amanda Benton." Edie hurried back with the information. "Do you know her?"

"I think so, but not by that last name. I'd like to buy this whole box." I picked it up and set it aside. "What will you take for it?"

"Oh, gee, Anabelle. I hate to ask anything for it since they're personal items. Oh, how about five dollars?"

"That's great, Edie. Thank you. I'll come back another day to look at the tablecloths."

I carried the box to my car and drove home. At my apartment, I looked carefully through all of the items in the box. All of it was Gary's property. How in the world had it ended up in an antique shop?

Even if he'd discarded it himself it would've been a reckless thing to do. Gary's parents would surely have been interested in keeping the stuff. Or even his children.

I phoned Jenny to see if she'd read or heard anything about Gary and Amanda Light breaking up. It had been a long time since I'd asked about Gary, so to explain why I told her that I ran across some things in Fabulous Finds that concern them.

Jenny was busy getting ready for dinner guests and didn't have much time to talk. "I do remember hearing something back, oh, maybe a year ago. It was something about the divorce of one of the Benton heirs. Maybe it was Amanda and Gary. Do you think?" Jenny perked up at the idea.

"Could be. I'll tell you all about why I'm asking another time. I know you're busy now." I let her go.

I was glad that I didn't have to analyze the news with Jenny right then. I wanted to sort it out privately. I was ashamed of myself. I was a grown woman and there I was with butterflies jumping hurdles in my stomach at the thought of a long, lost boyfriend getting divorced.

The more I pondered it over the weekend, the more I knew what I intended to do to get to the bottom of it. Monday morning I'd phone Gary's mother.

Ten-thirty will be a good time to call Mrs. Light, I decided. That's not too early and not too close to lunch.

I'd already looked the phone number up in the phonebook. It and the address were the same. I closed the door to my office and punched in the number. The night before I'd rehearsed what I was going to say.

"Mrs. Light." It was she who answered. I recognized her voice even though it had been eons since I last heard it.

"I don't know if you remember me or not, but this is Anabelle Connolly. I went to high school with Gary." I paused to let her answer.

"Oh, Anabelle! Of course I remember you! My goodness, what a surprise." She sounded delighted.

"It's good to hear your voice, Mrs. Light. I hope you're well."

"Yes, I am." She was polite, but query hung in her voice.

"The reason why I'm calling is because I came across some things of Gary's in a shop in town and I thought they may have been brought there by mistake." I proceeded to explain the situation in between Mrs. Light's occasional interjections of "Oh," and "I see."

When I was finished she said she was certain that Gary had no intention of throwing away those items and she definitely wanted to get the keepsakes back to him. She thanked me heartily several times.

I told her I'd bring them over to her house on Saturday, if that was all right. She was grateful and then asked me to tell her about myself.

That didn't take long. She seemed genuinely pleased to hear that I was happy, doing well, and excelling in my career.

It was my turn, and the obvious question was, "How's Gary?"

"He's doing okay, Anabelle. He's been through a tough time lately, but he's better now and I think he'll be all right. I'm ashamed to say it, but I suspect that it was Amanda, Gary's ex-wife, who got rid of his things. Just like she got rid of him."

Immediately, Mrs. Light regretted her indiscretion. "Oh, I'm sorry. That was a caddy thing to say. I'm sorry; please forget I said that."

"Don't worry. I've already forgotten," I replied.

"They divorced about a year or so ago. It wasn't pleasant."

I couldn't have been more excited if someone had said I'd won the lottery.

"They have a lovely little girl named Trina. She's my only grandchild and she's paying a price for the divorce." She couldn't disguise her bitterness.

After a few more niceties, we ended our conversation. She said she'd tell Gary that I called and that she looked forward to seeing me on Saturday.

So, Gary was divorced from Amanda. I was happy. I was sad. I was smug.

But what did I care? What did this really mean to me? Why was I working myself up into a state of anxiety over an old high school romance?

You're being juvenile, I reprimanded myself and then delved into the pile of paperwork on my desk.

But I continued to wonder about Gary. Did he live in Westside? Was he still working for the Benton Company? Where was his daughter? Was Gary heartbroken over his divorce or relieved? I didn't have the answers to any of those questions.

It would've been rude of me to ask Mrs. Light about any of it and I sensed that she felt a twinge of disloyalty to Gary when she told me as much as she did about his private life. Still, over the past few days I'd thought of little else but Gary.

Tuesday evening when I got home from work there was a message on my answering machine from Gary. I played it back three or four times. I didn't erase it. "Anabelle, this is Gary Light," stated the voice on the machine. "Mother said you called her. You have a box of things that are mine, she said. I'd be glad to come to your place to pick them up. It'll save you the trouble.

Call me at 693-0427. Oh, by the way—I found your number in the phonebook. At least I think it's yours. Thanks."

His voice sounded much as I remembered it, only stronger and deeper. It brought back a lot of sweet memories. The bad ones, I pushed out of my mind.

I waited till eight-thirty that night to call him. That left enough time to be through with dinner while it was still too early for bed. I took a deep breath and punched in the number. It was a Westside number. My heart was pounding when he answered.

"Gary, this is Anabelle Connolly. I got your message." I literally had to grab my right arm with my left hand to hold the phone steady.

"I did get the right number, then. I was hoping it was yours."

"I guess your mother told you why I called." I was trying to sound relaxed, but it was difficult with Gary on the other end of the line.

Apparently I didn't sound too weird because he said he'd come the following night to pick up the box of stuff.

Upon hearing the dull clang of the knocker and pausing for a few seconds to compose myself, I opened the door.

There he stood. He was a little heavier and there were a few streaks of gray at his temples. Instead of the youthful, cropped style, his hair was longer, parted, and combed—more befitting a business man. But he still had the same olive skin and that same bewitching smile. His casual clothes and easy manner should've calmed me, but my innards were bubbling in that way I hadn't felt in over a decade—not since the last time I was so close to Gary Light.

"Hello." I smiled back at him, a little awkward and a little shy. "Come in." I stepped aside to let him enter.

He glanced around the room, his eyes falling quickly back on me. "Wow!" he said and then hesitated. "It's great to see you. You look the same—only better." He blushed.

"Thanks. You do, too."

"No. Not really." He touched his waist and his temples and then laughed. "Nice of you to say, though."

The crinkles around his eyes and the sparkles in them sent me reeling. "Please, sit down." I gestured toward the couch. The box of stuff was on the floor beside it. "Would you like a glass of red wine?" I asked.

"Sure, thanks."

We sat on the couch side-by-side for two hours talking, sipping wine, and becoming reacquainted. By the end of the evening I was more in love with Gary than I had been at seventeen, though I tried to hide that revelation from him.

He seemed as warm and as charming and as interested in me as I'd hoped. Only his life was more complicated because of the responsibilities of being a husband and father. He carried more of the weight of the world on his shoulders.

Still, he couldn't conceal his sincere joy at seeing me again. He easily told me of his life over the past ten years. He talked about his love for his daughter, Trina, and his disdain for Amanda. The marriage had never been good, he admitted, but they'd made an effort for Trina's sake. That is, until it became a useless joke.

Gary didn't come right out and tell me that night that Amanda had cheated on him during their marriage, but that's what I deduced from the conversation. Anyway, she'd been married to someone else for close to a year, Gary said. Her new husband is a wealthy man who flies from one of his business enterprises to another. "He's much more suited to Amanda than I ever was," Gary said, placing his wine glass on the coffee table. "Only I worry about Trina. Amanda has custody of her, though she's free to visit me anytime. I guess the good part is just that—Trina stays with me a lot when Amanda's out jet-setting around." He rallied at the thought of his daughter and his dark eyes held mine again. "Have you heard enough?"

"No, please, don't stop." I almost gasped at the thought of ending this story in the middle. "Where do you live? Where do you work?" I couldn't contain my eagerness.

He told me that he was renting a cabin in the country about ten miles outside of Westside. After the chaos of the divorce and changing jobs, he wanted a quiet place to collect his thoughts, he said. And it's a two bedroom. Trina has a room of her own when she stays with him. And it's near enough to his mother so that Trina can spend time with her, too.

As for his job, well, when he and Amanda divorced he left his position at her father's company. He wanted a clean break from everything Benton, he said. He's an engineer now with the local water authority. He likes the work and the people he works with much better. "I know I'm making it on my own merit and not because I'm married to the boss' daughter. "The money's not as good," he continued. "But, hey, I don't need that much anymore."

In between Gary telling me about his life since high school, I told him about mine. "You've done well for yourself, Anabelle. I'm not surprised at that!" he exclaimed. "I'm a little surprised that you never married, though."

I sipped the last of my wine and placed the glass on the table beside Gary's. "I'm a bit surprised myself. But I never found a man

I wanted to be with forever."

A comfortable silence fell across the room as we mulled over everything we'd told each other.

"Here's the box of your things," I finally broke the quiet, pushing the box next to him.

He reached inside of it and tugged out a couple of photos. "Haven't seen these in a while." He lifted out his senior picture, which was still in the shattered glass frame. "Amanda did this. She took an ice pick to my forehead." He half grinned and half frowned. "Don't need to say anymore about that, I guess."

Then he reached in and took out his annual.

"How long has it been since you looked at it?" I asked.

"A looong time," he drawled. "But I never forgot one special page."

He turned directly to where my picture appeared, fixed his eyes on mine and recited from memory, "I'll never forget you. Anabelle." He lifted the book to his lips as he kissed my signature, just as he had all those years before.

He put down the annual and reached for my hands. He was so sexy and sensual. My heart was soaring.

"I've never forgotten you. Gary," he murmured. Then he kissed me gently. Afterward, he drew back slowly.

"Wow!" I whispered.

"Wow!" he echoed. And then he kissed me once more.

In case you haven't guessed, we're a couple again. We're taking our time with the hope of getting it right.

I adore Trina. She's sweet and easy to be with, just like her dad.

Amanda is no problem. She's so wrapped up in her new world that she lets Trina stay with Gary anytime she wants.

The three of us are already a family unto ourselves. Trina loves her mother, of course, but I can tell that she loves me, too.

When Gary and I are alone together, we're awed by the wonder of fate—Amanda discarded Gary's keepsakes at Fabulous Finds and I retrieved them.

Yet, it must be true. If a man and a woman are meant to be together, it'll happen.

THE END

WEEKEND IN THE WOODS
It saved my soul—and my marriage!

The silence that enveloped us as we drove home was broken only by the hum of the tires on the road. Silence was so common between my husband and me those days that it should've felt normal, but instead, the strain made me tense.

Turning my head to look out the window, I attempted to block out everything except the shadows racing past. The tension between us brought back memories that my mind had a hard time ignoring.

After five blissful years of marriage, our relationship hurt like an open wound. Trevor was busy building his architectural business while I crunched numbers at a local accounting firm. Low interest rates and increased building meant that Trevor's business was booming. I'd hoped the past year would be my last spent working for a while so Trevor and I could start the family we'd always wanted. I swallowed the lump of tears welling in my throat. It's a good thing that I never got pregnant because our lives had changed drastically since the accident.

Not wanting to rehash the most horrible event in my life, I forced my breath to move in and out, clearing my mind and willing myself to rest.

A hand caressed my hair. "Is everything okay, hon?" Trevor asked.

"Sure," I said, not wanting to talk about how tough I'd found the visit with my mom. Those days I dreaded contact with everyone close to me. Their pitying looks were even harder to take than those of strangers.

Trevor's hand rested on my shoulder until I pulled away. Why can't he just keep his hands on the wheel? I wondered.

"Why don't you sleep on the way home? Get some rest." I could hear the concern in his voice. My sleep had been sketchy ever since I finished my pain-pill prescription. Sleeping pills are too easy to get hooked on, so I avoided them. Instead, I stayed tired all the time, and the lack of sleep didn't help my state of mind.

Without a word, I sighed and let myself relax against the cool glass of the window. Even pretending to sleep was better than facing the questions hidden in the silence.

Soon the rhythm of the driving lulled me into a real sleep. I wasn't aware of anything else until Trevor cut the motor. The end of the soothing vibrations woke me up and I stared into complete

31

darkness. It was disorienting because I expected to see the glare of the garage light. "Trevor," I said, for once reaching out to him. "I think the garage light blew."

He chuckled. "The light isn't out, hon. We aren't in the garage. In fact, we aren't at home."

I sat up a little straighter, unease creeping in. Where else could we be so late at night? I wondered.

"Where are we?" I finally asked.

"Well, hon. . . ." He went quiet for a moment, then switched on the headlights with a click.

On the edge of the beam of light I could make out a covered, redwood deck attached to the front of a log cabin. Any other time the sight would've made me think of lazy afternoons spent reading in the cozy rocking chair while the sun shined through the sky, but right then all I could imagine was the solitude. Trevor and I—alone.

"What are we doing here?" Even I could hear the panic in my voice, but I couldn't hold it back. I wasn't ready for this. "Why aren't we at home?"

Oh, why didn't I stay awake? I wondered. Then I would've known what was going on and I could've stopped it.

"Trevor!" I demanded. "Answer me!"

His hands reached out of the dark and clasped mine. "Annemarie, calm down," he said in a tone that was meant to soothe me. "The cabin belongs to a friend of mine. I wanted to surprise you. We could both use some time away."

Surprise me! Yeah, right. He didn't tell me because he knew I wouldn't have come! Well, I wasn't going to stand for that. It was just plain inconsiderate.

My panic grew. Trevor and I could hardly spend an evening together in the same house in separate rooms, much less an entire weekend alone in this tiny cabin with no civilization for miles from the little I could see. "Trevor." I drew in a shaky breath for control. "Take me home—now."

Trevor released my hands and paused for a moment. Then he turned off the headlights and got out of the car. I sat there, stunned for a moment and then frantically felt around for the keys.

Where are they? I wondered. He must have them in his pocket.

Jumping out of the car, I accosted Trevor on the porch. "I said, take me home."

He faced me, his frustration coming out in a huff of air. "No." I could hear the firmness in his tone.

"What do you mean, no?"

"Just what I said. No."

"You kidnapped me!"

He grabbed my arms. "Annemarie, we can't go on like this. You know that. You've pulled away from me and gone to a place where I can't reach you anymore."

I couldn't tell him the truth; I couldn't let him see the fear and the ugliness both inside and outside of me.

He went on, "I feel like I'm losing you and I can't let that happen." One of his hands cupped my cheek. "I won't."

I shivered in the cool mountain air. I wasn't ready for this. He unlocked the door.

"We're staying here until we work this out."

That night I retreated to the only bedroom in the cabin. My eyes stayed glued to the doorknob for what felt like hours waiting to see if Trevor would open the firmly shut door, but I awoke the next morning to bright sunlight and an empty bed. Trevor must've slept on the couch.

Part of me was relieved, but another part of me was sad. I missed the warmth of my husband's arms wrapped around me. I wanted his comfort and support, but for that I'd have to let him in close—too close.

Smelling food, I decided to get dressed and confront Trevor again over breakfast. I thought maybe if I complained enough he'd give in to my demands.

I walked cautiously to the table and slid into a seat just as Trevor placed a plate piled high with bacon and pancakes in the middle of the table. He'd gotten to be a pretty good cook since my accident.

"Good morning," he said, leaning forward slightly like he intended to kiss my forehead.

"Morning," I murmured, disappointed as he pulled back. What's wrong with me? I wondered. Why can't I stay immune to this man?

As we ate in silence, I thought about my reaction. That was probably the reason I hadn't asked for a divorce. As afraid as I was of renewing the intimacy in our relationship, I loved Trevor so much that I didn't want to let go.

We finished the meal in the same silence in which we ate it. I wandered through the tiny cabin—which didn't take long— looking at the practical furniture that was touched up with feminine accents. There were enough of them to keep it from looking sparse, but not so many that the interior looked fussy. Gingham curtains covered the windows, a few pillows softened the futon couch, and a matching tablecloth dressed up the kitchen.

I settled into the rocking chair on the front porch, hoping the magnificent view would soothe my frazzled nerves. Trevor's following gaze didn't help. He seemed to be waiting for me to speak.

Well, I wasn't going to give him the satisfaction. This little trip was his idea. Let him make the first move, I thought.

I took in the colorful fall scenery, soaking in the beauty of nature. I didn't get to enjoy much of it in my accounting job, but at least I still had a job after my three-month absence to recover from the car accident.

Suddenly Trevor stood up. "How about a walk? Steve said the view from the top of that hill is spectacular."

I looked at the steep incline doubtfully, but anything had to be better than just sitting there.

We started up the wide trail. It was obvious that the owners used it frequently. Someone had taken the time to clear it and lay down a pine-needle covering to keep the weeds out. Still, I moved slower with each step. An ache that began in my ankle had stretched up my leg and into my stomach by the time we reached the top. But I pushed on, just as I had through hundreds of hours of physical therapy, by reminding myself to be grateful that I could walk at all.

The view from the top really was worth the climb. Trevor's friend had told the truth. I took a deep breath of the crisp air and looked over the valley below that nestled the little cabin in its depths.

The little home looked snug and serene. It's the perfect place for a weekend getaway for a husband and wife who want to renew their relationship with quality time together, I thought. I turned away from the pain the image brought me.

Starting toward a fallen log to rest my leg, my muscles gave way and I fell to the ground.

"Annemarie!" Trevor yelled, hurrying to my side. "Are you okay?"

Without waiting for an answer, he scooped me up from the ground and carried me to the log. He set me down with a tender touch. "My God, Annemarie, I'm sorry. I should've thought about your leg before suggesting that we walk so far. Let me check it out."

The gentle touch of his hands as they slid up my leg checking for injuries made me wish for the feel of those same hands against my bare skin. I wanted them to touch me in passion rather than concern, but those times would never come again—not if I had the self-control to prevent it. I pulled away firmly.

Trevor sat back on his heels and met my gaze with shadows in his eyes. "You blame me, don't you?"

I blinked in confusion. "No, I wanted to take a walk."

He shook his head. "I mean, you blame me for the accident."

The blood drained from my brain, leaving me lightheaded. Had he spent all those months thinking I held him responsible?

"You aren't the only one, Annemarie. I blame myself just as much. I second-guess every moment of our ride. I was behind the wheel. I should've been more aware and seen that guy coming. If I had, I could've turned the car and he wouldn't have rammed into your side." His voice broke, but he pushed the rest of the words out. "I would've taken it on me, all of it, rather than hurt one hair on your head."

The pain in his voice and the tears in his eyes broke my resolve for the first time since I'd realized the full extent of the damage the accident had done to me. I reached for my husband and put my arms around his shoulders as he knelt before me. Leaning close, I savored the feel of him and the touch I'd refused myself. I'd missed him so much during those last few lonely months.

"I'm sorry," I whispered close to his ear. What we went through and were still going through was bad enough without the burden of guilt Trevor had secretly carried on his broad shoulders. I sandwiched his handsome face between my shaking hands and buried my fingers in his thick, dark hair. "I don't blame you at all. I have never. . . ." I swallowed the lump in my throat. Looking him in the eye was harder than looking at my new reflection in the mirror. "Neither of us saw it coming. There was nothing you could've done, even if you had warning. These things just happen."

I cringed inside as I heard the same words that were said to me in the hospital leave my mouth. He needed assurance of my feelings, not words to cover up the guilt. "You're not responsible for this. I've never thought that and never will. The idiot who decided to get behind the wheel drunk did this to me. And I couldn't have gotten this far without your love and support."

He still looked troubled. "But I don't understand. If you don't hold me responsible, then why the cold shoulder? Why do you refuse to let me hold you and touch you?" He squeezed me tight. "Like this."

Closing my eyes, I savored the pressure of his arms for a moment before pulling away with a sigh. "Trevor, I'm honestly not able to deal with anything else right now." I rushed on when his face fell, "I need the rest of my strength to get down this mountain. Can we talk about this tomorrow, please?"

I could tell that he was disappointed, but it didn't show in his gentle touch as he helped me to my feet. Not giving me a chance to object, he tucked my arm around his waist and placed his hand over mine. "Lean on me," he said.

With his help, I was able to make it back to the cabin. Once there, I headed for the bathroom. "I'm going to take a hot bath." Dealing with countless sore muscles and cramping had taught me that a hot bath would ease both after overuse.

Trevor's voice stopped me. "Why don't you try the hot tub?"

I turned, frowning. "What hot tub?"

He responded with a mischievous grin. "The one on the back porch."

The thought was tempting. I could just feel the warm, bubbling water covering me, inch-by-inch, easing away my every ache and pain. I could imagine Trevor joining me. In my mind, we created steam that had nothing to do with the hot water. I could practically feel his hands on my back and my stomach, then sliding across my thighs. . . .

I snatched my thoughts away with a moan. No way could I put myself in the middle of so much temptation. It wasn't right for me and it wasn't fair to him. "I can't; I don't have a swimsuit," I said, clutching at the first excuse that came to me.

Trevor stepped closer. "I came totally prepared. Your swimsuit is in the suitcase."

I knew which one it would be. He wouldn't have packed the plain, black one-piece. Oh, no. Trevor was all man. He would've gone straight for the hot pink bikini hiding at the back of my underwear drawer that I'd taken on our few trips together. I'd rather die than let him compare the new me to his memories of me in this swimsuit on the beach in the Bahamas, I thought.

I searched frantically for another excuse. "Maybe I'll take a nap, instead. I'm rather tired."

Pain entered his eyes, causing me to wince. I didn't want to hurt him, but I had, anyway. Our relationship needed to end before I hurt him anymore. I hadn't found the strength to do it yet, but the forced time alone showed me more than the last three months how awful I was for him.

Making good on my lame excuse, I spent the rest of the afternoon and early evening sleeping. For once, it wasn't a waste of time. Instead, it kept me from dwelling too much on my problems and gave my body a rest.

I awoke once more to the smell of food. This time it was lasagna, my favorite dinner. Guilt gripped me heavy and strong and I straightened, forcing myself to face it. I just had to get through the weekend. At home I could return to the comfort of my solitary room and avoid being alone with Trevor.

Scaredy cat, I lectured myself.

I made my way to the kitchen. Trevor glanced up as I walked

in the room. "Good, you're awake. Dinner's almost ready."

Deciding I should be more social and kind, I attempted neutral conversation. After all, he'd gone to a lot of trouble for his pitiful excuse for a wife. "Did you make this yourself?" I asked, indicating the pan of bubbling cheese and tomato sauce.

He grinned. "Sure, I opened the box and popped it in the oven."

It smelled so good I decided to overlook that. "Cheater!"

"Hey, I was hoping to spend my weekend doing more than cooking."

The teasing abruptly changed to sadness. Pretending not to notice, I sat in a chair and began to serve the salad. After we spent a few moments absorbed in the food, Trevor cleared his throat.

"Annemarie, I realize that all of this has been very difficult for you, but I hope you realize that I had the best of intentions bringing you here."

The lasagna lodged in my throat, forcing me to swallow hard. "Of course I do."

He reached out for my hand. "I love you. I don't want to lose you."

You already have, I thought. You lost me the minute that drunk slammed into our car and ruined me.

I tried to pull away, but he gripped me tighter. "No, Annemarie. I'm not going to let you run away anymore. I want you to tell me what's wrong. If you don't blame me, then why are you pulling back from me? Have I not helped enough? Been supportive enough? What?"

I wanted to slap my hands over my ears, but I couldn't break his grip. "No, Trevor. I told you—it's me. You haven't done anything wrong."

"Then talk to me."

"I can't!" The words burst from my chest. "I won't. I'll never be the same again. Just leave me alone!" The words ended on a sob.

He jerked back as if I'd hit him. "Fine," he said, his voice clipped. He walked out the door without looking back and I knew I'd hurt him terribly. All the patience he'd showered me with those past months was at an end and I couldn't blame him. I could blame no one but myself.

What is wrong with me? I wondered. Am I willing to give up everything because I'm afraid to expose the scars and show Trevor the ugly side of me?

I was being so selfish. I could finally see that. Only a man who loved deeply would go to the trouble of kidnapping his wife to save their marriage. That took a lot of courage on his part, especially after the way I behaved. Could I give him any less? The answer was no.

But I couldn't imagine how to open the subject again. I'd hurt Trevor. How could I approach him so he'd listen? I trembled at the thought. What will I do if he hates me?

I heard a dragging sound on the back porch and crossed to the window to look out. I caught a glimpse of Trevor lowering himself into the shadowy depths of the hot tub, his body collapsing into the seat as if he could no longer carry his heavy burden.

Just then, an idea blossomed in my mind. With slowly quickening steps, I walked to the bedroom. Rummaging through the suitcase, I found the swimsuit in the back—the pink bikini. I allowed myself a brief smile despite the rapidly mounting tension. Men can be so predictable, I thought.

With shaking hands, I stripped my clothes off and pulled on the suit without giving myself time to think about what I was doing. I kept my eyes averted from the angry, red scars that formed a prickly patchwork up my right thigh and side. Trevor's display of courage meant that I could do no less than meet him with my own. I'd show him everything and let the choice be his.

Snagging a towel, I wrapped it around my waist on the way to the back door. I killed the lights in the kitchen and plunged the back porch into shadows. There was no need to make it harder than it already was for me.

Stepping quietly onto the back porch, my stomach lurched as Trevor turned his head my way. I couldn't read his expression, but I knew that he was wondering what I wanted.

"Mind if I join you?" I asked.

I could feel his shock. I approached the tub slowly, dreading the moment I'd be close enough for him to see me clearly. As I stepped into the moonlight, Trevor stood. I paused for a moment. Then I forced myself to move closer, easing the towel farther down with each step.

With my eyes adjusted to the dimmer light, I could see his eyes linger on the top that showcased my breasts. A brief glimmer of pleasure flared in the midst of my nervousness and pain. I felt so vulnerable. My instinct was to turn and run, but I remained still as his eyes dropped lower, widening slightly as they first skimmed and then came back to linger on the scars. I cringed inside but kept my body totally still.

He'd never seen the full extent of the damage and he needed to if we were ever going to move on from there. "Oh, Annemarie," he said as he climbed out of the tub. Standing before me, he reached out and ran his fingertips lightly over the scars at my waist.

"Oh, Annemarie, I'm so sorry."

He knelt before me and feather kissed his way down my right side. His touch wasn't passionate, but I recognized a tender reverence that brought tears to my eyes. Then he helped me into the bubbling water. He pulled me into his arms, his touch firm like he expected me to pull away and he wasn't about to give me the chance. "Annemarie, why didn't you show me before? Do you think I'm so shallow that I wouldn't love you, scars and all?"

I struggled to put into words what I'd only just come to realize. "I told myself it would bother you, but I think the truth is that I'm the one who couldn't face you seeing me and exposing myself to your pity and pain. I wanted to protect myself."

"So, all this time, that's why you wouldn't let me hold you and touch you?"

"I didn't trust myself to keep you at a distance emotionally if you were touching me."

His arms tightened around me and he chuckled. "I'll have to remember that in the future." He frowned. "We do have a future, don't we? That's what this means, right, Annemarie?"

I lay my head on his shoulder. "That isn't the only reason why I stayed away from you, Trevor. I may be superficial, but I'm not that vain."

"What is it?"

"Trevor, what if I'm not able to have children?"

"The doctor said that your internal organs weren't permanently damaged."

"Yes, but my leg is. No matter how much therapy I do, I'll always limp and have pain. What if I can't handle pregnancy, giving birth, and all of the carrying and running that goes along with being a mother?"

He framed my face with his hands. "We'll do whatever it takes to make it easier. And I'll be right there beside you—hands on and involved. We'll do it together."

As his strong arms held me that night, I knew that we would.

Now we are closer than we've ever been in our relationship. Trevor began working from home to care for our baby, who is now a rambunctious toddler. He was with me every step of the pregnancy and we raise her together.

Therapy has helped me face the physical challenges of pregnancy. My limp is barely noticeable anymore and I only hurt when I overdo it. Life is good, even with a kidnapper for a husband.

THE END

THE BOTHERED BRIDE
I took a vow of loyalty—not loneliness!

When I told Mom that Drew asked me to the senior prom she reacted just as I expected her to—she stood in the middle of our kitchen and ordered me not to go with him. "Drew Hanson! How can you even think of dating a guy like that, Eva?"

"He's one of those Hansons who live on the other side of town in that trailer park! I doubt that his father has ever worked an honest day in his life and I heard that his sister has a baby already and she isn't even married. You don't need to get mixed up with a bunch of losers like that, Eva."

But I knew that I was already "mixed up" with Drew—in my heart, in my mind, and in my thoughts. His handsome face and the sight of his tall, slender body filled my every waking—and sleeping—moment. Yes, I was mixed up with Drew and that was exactly the way I wanted it to be.

We were in many of the same classes the last few years of high school. We also spent time studying together in the library and ate lunch together. During that time, I realized that Drew was the man who I wanted to spend my life with and I knew that he felt the same way about me. I wished Mom would've listened to me when I tried to tell her what a wonderful person he is, but she just turned and walked away, muttering something about "that worthless Hanson clan." I knew that it was a wasted effort to try to make her understand that going to the prom with Drew was very important to me, so I didn't discuss it with her any further.

I went to the prom with Drew and it felt so wonderful to dance to the music with his arms wrapped around me. He told me a hundred times that he loved me, and the look in his chocolate eyes said more than words ever could. That night, before he drove me home, he asked me to marry him. Graduation was only one week away and we knew that our lives would be headed in a new direction.

My best friend, Jill, and I talked often about what would happen to us after we finished school. She knew that she loved her boyfriend, Kenny, and I knew that I loved Drew. When he proposed, I eagerly told Drew I'd marry him. As he held me close under the warm, summer sky, I felt happier than I ever had before.

When I got home and told Mom that I was going to marry Drew, she really threw a fit. But I expected it. I let her rant and rave and recite her long list of things that she thought were wrong with Drew. I just sat there and concentrated on everything that was right about him. I thought about the ambition he had to better himself and move out of the trailer park. He already had a part-time job at a warehouse, and after graduation he was going to work there full-time. He wasn't lazy like Mom insisted that he was; he had ambition and hope for a bright future. I wanted to be a part of his dreams and his future.

When I talked to Jill the day after the prom, she told me that she'd agreed to marry Kenny. Although her parents fussed some about it, they didn't give her a ton of static. They did, however, try to get her to wait a year before tying the knot to make sure that Kenny was the right man for her.

"I know that my parents are just trying to protect me," Jill said, "but I also know that Kenny is the right man for me. I have no intention of waiting a whole year to be his wife. So, next weekend we're going across the state line to get married! In fact, I think it would be great if you and Drew came with us. We're all of legal age, so we can do that, you know. We could have a double wedding! Think how exciting that would be!"

And that's just how it happened. On a sunny June morning the four of us piled into Kenny's secondhand car, drove across the state line, and in a matter of hours Jill was Mrs. Kenny Rutherford and I was Mrs. Andrew Hanson. I was thrilled.

Mom, of course, blew a gasket. She threatened to have the marriage annulled, but I told her that if she did that I'd never set foot in her house again. I knew that my life was meant to be spent with Drew. I wanted Mom to be a part of my happiness, but she just turned her back on me and left me standing on the front porch holding my suitcases. I'd just removed some of my belongings from my old bedroom and she didn't even say good-bye.

Drew's parents were thrilled when they found out that we got married and they immediately considered me a part of their family. His sister, Dina, instantly became the sister I never had. Her two-year-old little boy, Eric, was adorable and kept insisting that I hold him as we sat in their trailer and drank glasses of orange soda.

I found Ma, Drew's mom, to be charming and pretty in spite of the fact that she was somewhat overweight. She worked at a local bakery and I think she sampled the product a little too much. Dina worked at a nearby convenience store. Pa Hanson had been badly injured in a trucking accident some years earlier and wasn't able to work, so he took care of little Eric while Dina worked. Each of them contributed to the family in their own way. There was a bond between them that I never had with Mom or with my dad before a heart attack took him several years before.

Drew and I rented a trailer several spaces down from his parents' trailer and settled into our new life. I got a job at the local library and loved being a working girl. I especially loved being the wife of the most wonderful man in the world.

I could hardly believe it when Drew and I celebrated out first anniversary. Several months later, Drew was offered a promotion at work. His boss, Phil, wanted Drew to learn more about the inner workings of the warehouse. He recognized Drew's ambition and willingness to work hard to try to improve an already successful business. I was so proud of my husband because I knew he'd earned that promotion.

We went to a nice restaurant that night to celebrate and discuss our future. He ordered a wonderful meal for us that included drinks. I never touch alcoholic beverages, but he seemed to enjoy having a few of what he called his "specialties." It seemed appropriate since it was a special occasion.

He was going to be earning more money and I already earned a good salary working at the library, so we felt it was the right time to begin house hunting. We looked forward to moving into a home of our own and bought a ranch house several blocks from where Jill and Kenny had purchased a place of their own.

Our house needed some repairs, but we got it at a reduced price. We spent many hours painting bedrooms, replacing worn-out carpet in the living room, and refinishing the kitchen cabinets. It was a lot of hard work, but we enjoyed every minute of the time we spent turning our house into a home by adding our own personal touches to it.

Since we owned our own home, we hoped that my mom would come to visit us. She'd never been to our trailer and I felt badly about that. I really enjoyed the closeness between Ma, Pa, Dina, and Drew and I. We were a real family. We laughed together, shared good moments, and leaned on each other during difficult times. We were always there for each other. I wished that Mom would agree to meet Ma and Pa and get to know them. Then she'd see that they're kind, caring, hardworking people. But she never called me or came to see us and I didn't feel welcome in her house. When I occasionally phoned her in an effort to rebuild some sort of relationship, she'd hardly speak to me. More than once I sat and cried after talking to her on the phone.

Since we now had a house instead of a trailer, I thought that perhaps Mom would come to see our home and spend some time with us. I know that she cringed at the notion of going to a trailer to visit, but I was sure that she'd be willing to come to our nice house. She'd recently sold the house that she and Dad owned together—the house I grew up in. She moved into an apartment complex and from what I could gather she liked her new place and was making friends with some of the other people who lived there. She'd made a new life for herself and I didn't feel like I was included in it. But there was a part of me that still loved her and still hoped that things would change between us.

Phil was pleased with the progress Drew was making in his new position. He asked Drew if he'd like to move out of the warehouse part of the business and get involved with the computers that had recently been installed to make the overall work process more efficient. Drew was eager to learn new skills, and so when Phil offered to send Drew to evening classes at the local community college, he jumped at the chance.

That meant that Drew worked all day long and then spent several evenings per week in class. He was so busy that we seldom spent any time together. There were evenings when I sat home alone trying to get interested in some program on TV, but all I could think about was how much I missed my husband. I was really proud of him for the way he was applying himself and working and studying around the clock, but somewhere in there our relationship seemed to come to a standstill.

I was left alone so much that I started spending more and more time at the trailer with Ma and Pa and Dina. They became my real family. Ma shared some of her family recipes with me, Pa challenged me to battles of Chinese Checkers that he usually won, and Dina and I went to yard sales looking for clothes for Eric. That boy was really growing and I enjoyed watching his progress as he started preschool and then went on to kindergarten.

I also spent time with Jill. She and Kenny were by then the proud parents of a son and a daughter. She's extremely proud of her children and I'm overjoyed to be their aunt Eva. Jill and I sometimes took the kids to the mall or to the park. Other times, she and I would sit and sip tea while we watched the little ones play on the living room rug. She seemed so happy and so fulfilled and I was so thrilled for her.

Drew and I spent almost no time together. He no longer had time to work on the small garden beside our garage and he'd really enjoyed tending to the plants the previous year. He'd been so proud of the tomatoes and green beans and carrots that he grew all by himself. Now the space that had produced those beautiful vegetables was a weed patch. Our lawn seldom got mowed properly because he simply didn't have time for things like home maintenance.

43

I tried not to say anything about it because I knew that he was working hard and pushing himself. He didn't need to contend with a wife who nagged him to trim the hedges or repair the broken step on the back porch. I paid a neighbor boy to take care of the yard and Pa came over and replaced the step. He also fixed our leaky kitchen faucet.

Eventually, the evening classes ended and I figured that things would begin to settle down since Drew's entire day would no longer be fully loaded with "must do" things. For a few weeks, all he had to do was go to work and come home. There were no other obligations and no classes to sit through.

I was so happy to have my husband back with me. Just having him there made my heart sing. I realized that I loved him totally and I was glad that we could go back to being close like we were when we first got married.

We finally had a chance to go out to dinner and a movie. He went to the mall with me one day and another time we went to a summer festival in the park. We did all of the things that normal people who have normal routines do and I loved every moment that I spent with him. It was wonderful to work all day at the library and then come home and put a casserole in the oven and do some housework. When Drew got home, we'd have a nice meal together and then curl up on the sofa together and watch TV. We had a chance to reconnect. On the weekends, he cooked steaks on our outdoor grill and I made tossed salads and raspberry iced tea. I loved the tea, but Drew preferred several bottles of beer. That was okay with me as long as I had my wonderful husband all to myself.

I was happier than I'd been for quite some time, but after the first few weeks of the new routine, Drew seemed restless and unsettled. I guess because he'd been going at such a hectic pace for so long he found it difficult to settle down, relax, and just enjoy his home and his wife.

As if Phil hadn't taken enough of Drew's time, he decided to send my husband to a seminar in Chicago to upgrade his already upgraded computer skills. When Drew told me about the opportunity, he was animated and seemed very eager to go. Even though I didn't want him to go so far away for an entire week, I never told him so. I helped him pack his suitcase and gave him an extra kiss before I headed off to work at the library. I wanted to drive him to the airport, but I couldn't take the time off from work.

When I got home from work late the following Friday afternoon, I was surprised to find Drew sitting at the kitchen table drinking a cup of coffee. "I got an early flight home," he explained as he took a sip of his drink.

While I got a meal ready, he told me about the things he'd seen and done during the week. He told me about a couple of parties he went to, as well. They were just get-togethers for the people attending the seminar, but it sounded to me like he went on a grand vacation. Seeing him so pleased with his accomplishments during the seminar made me happy for him. For some reason, though, I also felt unhappy about the fact that I felt so shut out from his adventure.

Over dinner, he continued to tell me about how wonderful Chicago was. He never asked how I was doing or what kinds of things had happened to me while he was away. It was as though only his activities were important.

He's just wound up from all he saw and did this week, I told myself as I cleared away the dishes.

Now that he was back at home, I assumed that our life would settle down into a more regular pattern. Once again, I was wrong. Phil considered Drew his prize pupil. He began taking him to special meetings to meet a variety of people connected in one way or another with the warehouse. Often this occurred after working hours, so, once again, Drew was gone in the evenings. He'd often come home around midnight, exhausted from a long day. If he bothered to kiss me before heading into the shower, I knew that the meeting had included drinks. I guessed that was a part of climbing the corporate ladder.

I began to feel like I didn't even know my husband anymore. He was totally absorbed in his work and in getting ahead and climbing the ladder of success. I still worked in the children's department of the local library and I think he thought of my job as mediocre compared to his high-tech job. Actually, we really had very little to talk about those days because we were traveling on two different roads.

I was concerned about our relationship and about the communication between us. Actually, maybe I should say that I was concerned about the lack of communication between us—on any level. I felt like the man who lived in my house was a stranger to me. We shared the same address, the same last name, and the same bed—but that was it. We no longer laughed together, worked together, or played together. I was living with someone who I didn't even know.

I began to feel like Drew had outgrown me because he was learning more and more about computers. I used computers all the time at the library, but I knew that my use of computers didn't begin to compare with Drew's application of them. I began to feel inferior to him. After all, he was Phil's right-hand man and I was just a lowly librarian.

I also grew concerned about Drew's relationship with his family. He never went to see them at the trailer park—he just didn't have the time for something as simple as spending time with his mother, father, sister, and nephew.

I still went to be with them every chance I got. I loved spending time them, sharing meals, watching TV, and just sitting around chatting about anything or nothing at all. We'd just relax together as a family and Drew didn't have time for frivolous things like that.

There were several more trips out of town—one to New York and another to Florida. Phil started sending his office manager, a woman named Peggy, along, too. Drew no longer made the trips alone because Peggy occupied the seat beside him on the plane and the motel room next door.

After those trips, Drew began getting calls at home from Peggy. I could hear them—at least I could hear his end of the conversation—as they discussed different computer situations involving the office. The calls seemed like legitimate office work, but there was something about them that unnerved me. He was around Peggy all day at work, so why couldn't they manage to accomplish enough at the office without having to rehash a lot of computer stuff in the evenings?

Resentment was building up inside of me. Drew's a hardworking man—maybe too hard working. He tried to improve himself by going to evening classes and by going to seminars. How could I possibly fault a man for something like that? In fact, I was proud of all that he was accomplishing. Mom had said that Drew would never amount to anything. Well, he certainly was proving her wrong about that.

The rare evenings when he was home, he was so weary and tired that he'd just drop onto the sofa in front of the TV with the remote control in one hand and a can of beer in the other. Then he'd get lost in the football or baseball game on the screen. I tried to watch the games with him, thinking that if we shared a common interest such as sports it might help us connect. But I'd quickly lose interest in the game and head to the kitchen or the laundry room to tend to chores.

It was about that time that Mom and I started to talk on the phone more frequently. I'd always been the one to phone her, but then she started calling me occasionally. I finally got her to agree to come over to our house on a Saturday afternoon and she was surprised by how nice it was. It's nothing fancy, but it's a comfortable home. She sat in my kitchen and peeled apples as I prepared the crust for a pie. It was wonderful to have her there with me and for us to be involved in a simple task like baking an apple pie. I sent part of it home with her when she left. I felt bad that Drew wasn't there with us but, as usual, he was off doing some task at the warehouse. I wanted Mom to be able to spend time with him and get to know him so that she'd know what a special person he is.

It helped me that I had Ma, Pa, Dina, Jill and my own mom to keep me company. If it hadn't been for them, I would've felt totally alone. As it was, I felt almost totally separated from Drew. He was so caught up in his own pursuits that he rarely paid any attention to me those days.

And rumors that had started as whispers began to escalate. A couple of the girls at the library wondered about Drew's relationship with Peggy. I assured them that she was just a business acquaintance, but I could tell by their looks and the way they shrugged their shoulders as they turned away from me that they didn't agree.

I felt especially bad when I had to spend our anniversary by myself. Drew was away at a business meeting that Peggy was also required to attend.

Jill and Kenny had planned a romantic candlelight dinner to celebrate the anniversary date that Drew and I shared with them. I assured her that Drew and I would have a special evening of our own as soon as he returned from his business trip, but I could tell that Jill didn't really believe me. In truth, I didn't believe it, either. The only words I was beginning to believe were the ones swirling around me that hinted at Drew's unfaithfulness.

Still, I refused to accept the idea that he might be having an affair with Peggy. Drew just wasn't the kind of guy who'd do such a thing. Maybe we had run away to get married, but that didn't mean that we took our marriage vows any less seriously. We discussed that fact several times. When we pledged to be faithful to each other we meant every word of it. No, it just wasn't like Drew to cheat on me.

Just the same, things were beginning to point more and more in that direction. There was all the time he spent at work and all the time he spent with Peggy. He mentioned that she was divorced. He seemed to feel sorry for her and he considered her a helpless woman who was out on her own and trying to make a new life for herself. That was one reason why she worked so hard for Phil. Like Drew, she was determined to get ahead. He seemed to admire that in her and something about the way he said it made me feel like he felt that I wasn't ambitious and didn't have a strong enough desire to advance in my job. The fact that I was Assistant to the Director of the Children's Department at the library didn't impress him. After all, I was just working with children and that didn't compare to his working with computers and attending endless numbers of classes, seminars, and important business meetings.

I'm not sure exactly when the arguing started. For the first several years of our marriage, Drew and I seldom argued about anything. We occasionally had "discussions" where he'd voice his opinion about something and I'd explain my side of an issue, but we're both easygoing people and arguing isn't in our natures. Slowly but surely, though, arguments and disagreements began to erupt.

Usually Drew was the one who initiated it. He'd get angry because his favorite shirt hadn't been laundered or because he couldn't find the remote control for the TV. Sometimes he'd blow up because he couldn't find his favorite tie which he just had to wear to a business meeting. He owned tons of ties, but he often had to have that special one and when he couldn't find it one day he started hurling ties and shirts and shoes out of his closet in an effort to locate the special tie. He finally spied it on the back of a chair where he'd tossed it a few days earlier. I couldn't believe how angry he got. What's worse, he felt it was my fault that the tie wasn't on his tie rack in the closet.

I attributed Drew's bouts of anger to the fact that he was working harder than ever. Phil kept making more and demands on him. When I suggested that Drew turn down one of Phil's assignments, he got very agitated.

"Are you kidding, Eva? This is a great opportunity for me! Phil wants me to handle this account personally because he trusts me to do it and do it right! How can I tell him no when he could've easily asked Jake or Bill to handle it? He gave this to ME and there's no way I can turn him down!" Then he added in an accusing tone, "That is, unless you don't want me to get ahead in the company. Is that what this is all about? How can you be like that, Eva?"

I stood and watched as he ranted on and on about the wonderful opportunity he was being given thanks to Phil's generosity. I saw anger in his eyes. I also saw frustration and extreme exhaustion from trying to do too much in an endless struggle to please Phil.

"Drew, I'm not trying to keep you from getting ahead at the warehouse," I said. "I know you're making great progress and in

48

time you'll become a supervisor or a manager or get some other lofty position. I'm very proud of all that you've achieved. I don't know anyone else who could've risen so high in the company so fast. You've earned every promotion that Phil has given you, but to get there you are pushing too hard, working too hard, and literally wearing yourself out. You never have any time off, you never relax—"

"I relax!" he snapped at me.

"Yes? How?" I countered. I couldn't recall the last time he'd really been relaxed or at ease.

"Well . . . I-I stop at Frankie G's after work with a few of the guys and have a beer. We talk, unwind, and take it easy."

That was true. He was getting home from work later and later and staying at Frankie G's longer and longer. Often he came home too full of drink and Frankie G's greasy hamburgers to even bother to eat the good meal I'd prepared. Is that what he was calling relaxing? I guess in his estimation it was, since it usually ended up with him dropping onto the couch, grabbing the remote control, and sleeping through a football game or a science-fiction movie. I'd end up going to bed without him and I really didn't even care. I mean, who wants to sleep next to a guy who smells like a brewery?

The next morning he'd be off to work again—back to the grind of trying to please Phil in every way he could. The cycle went on and on, round and round, and somewhere in the center of it all was a marriage that was spiraling down into a dismal place filled with shadows and heartache and tears.

Jill and I have always been close. I always enjoyed being around her, but I began to resent it when she stopped by because she was always so happy, so upbeat, and so full of stories about her two wonderful kids and her wonderful husband, Kenny. She talked about the four of them having picnics in the park, cuddling up on the couch to watch cartoons together, building a playhouse in the backyard, and taking a vacation to the seashore. They never did anything fancy or costly because Kenny didn't earn much money at his job, but they did things together and they were a family.

Every time she left my house I felt like she'd just underlined every flaw and failure in my marriage. We had no children because Drew wanted to wait until he was more successful before taking on the responsibility of kids. We spent almost no time together— never went to the park or to dinner—and there was no way we could possibly find time for a vacation to the seashore or anywhere else. Jill's life was a sheet of notebook paper filled with the scribbles of little kids' crayons and the roughly sketched drawing for a home-made play house. Our life was one big, blank page.

I felt like I was living in a non-existent world. I was a wife without a husband living in a home that contained no love. What had gone wrong? Once, there'd been happiness in the house. There'd been activity and the fun of working side by side to create a home; there'd been loving moments of candlelight and soft music and tender touches. Now the rooms, just like my life, seemed empty. It was like no one lived in our house anymore.

I began to feel moments of anger at the most unlikely times. If I were at the mall and saw a couple walking along together, smiling and talking, I'd feel a flicker of rage start in the pit of my stomach and slither up my spine. If I prepared a good, wholesome meal and then had to sit and eat it alone at the kitchen table because Drew wasn't there—again—to share the meal with me, I'd feel frustrated and disappointed. He used to really like my meatloaf and now he wasn't even home to enjoy it with me. There were too many unshared meals and too many evenings alone that made me feel unwanted and abandoned.

My home life might've been a total zero, but my work at the library continued to bring me special moments. I loved being with the children and seeing their fascination with books and their keen interest in things, but I was having difficulty concentrating on my work. I began having headaches and my neck hurt, my back hurt, and my arms ached. When the headaches started happening more and more, I finally went to Dr. Coyle. But she could find nothing wrong with me.

"You're so tense, Eva," she looked at me with concern in her eyes. "Is something worrying you? Are there problems with your job? Your muscles are so tight, no wonder you hurt and ache and have headaches. Are you sleeping well?"

"Not really," I admitted. It had been a long while since I'd had a good night's sleep. Many nights Drew never even came home. Later, he'd explain that he had to work late so he just slept on the couch in the company lounge. I wanted to believe him, but I didn't. A big bed is a very lonely place when no one shares it with you. So many nights I got almost no sleep at all.

Dr. Coyle wrote me a prescription for something that was supposed to relax me, calm me, and help me to sleep. I thanked her and left her office. After filling the prescription at the pharmacy, I shoved the small, plastic bottle into a corner of my purse. I had no intention of taking any of those pills. No little pill was going to make me feel better and I doubted that I'd ever feel right again. I took aspirin for the headaches and took hot showers before bedtime to relax my tight muscles. Somehow, I got through the days—one day at a time.

When Drew was home, he always had some sort of alcoholic drink in his hand. That was something he never did when we were first married. He said that he needed a drink to relax after spending a day dealing with computers and customers and supervisors. He kept a supply of wine and other alcoholic beverages in the cupboard and made sure there was a nice supply of beer in the refrigerator.

I hated his drinking, but I didn't dare ask him to stop. The few times I tried, he angrily declared that it was his house, too, and that if he wanted to have a drink or two to help him relax after work then he would do just that! His tone and attitude left no room for debate. He wanted to drink and therefore he was going to drink. His outbursts startled and frightened me. They seemed to occur more frequently and I began to feel like I was walking on eggshells whenever I was around him. I didn't want to upset him or anger him; he wasn't violent, but I felt intimidated by him.

I finally felt that I could take no more. The wall that had built up between us was too high and too solid, and I had no idea how to begin to climb over it or tear it down. If ours was a normal marriage, then I wanted no part of marriage. My parents never had a perfect marriage, but they were kind, gentle, and considerate of each other. They showed me a good example of what marriage can be like. Drew's own parents are far from wealthy, but they're rich in love and laughter and tenderness. Drew, like me, grew up knowing what a good marriage looks like and there was nothing in our relationship that was even close to what our parents shared.

I finally had to admit that marrying Drew at such a young age—and against my mother's wishes and without her blessing—was a mistake. A very serious mistake. We were in love, but we were too young. We knew that we were meant to be together forever; we knew that our love was magic. Somewhere down through the years the magic of our love had faded and evaporated, leaving behind only emptiness, loneliness, and tears.

On a warm, autumn night I sat on the couch holding a framed photo of Drew and me taken just weeks after our runaway wedding. We both looked so happy; I could actually see the stars that shined in our eyes. I always kept that photo on the end table as a reminder of how wonderful our love was. Just then I held it out at arm's length, loving the photograph and yet hating it with such a loathing that I felt I was smothering. Sobs tore at my throat as I wept because I knew that things would never again be the way they used to be. I grieved for the wonderment and passion that we'd lost.

51

"No more!" I screamed to the silent room. "No more waiting for him to come home! No more feeling like he doesn't even know who I am anymore! No more wanting him and loving him and hating him! NO MORE!"

My sobs ceased and then I set the photo back on the end table, got up, and walked to the front window. As I stood looking out at the night sky, I saw a shooting star send a thin slice of light through the darkness. Mom used to tell me that any wish made upon a shooting star was sure to come true. Just as the star faded from view, I whispered, "I wish this marriage was over! I wish it had never happened!"

As I turned and moved from the window, I recalled Mom also telling me, "Be careful what you wish for—it just might come true."

A few days later Jill stopped by with some shocking news. She seldom managed to get away from her kids, but that day her mother-in-law had taken the children to the park so Jill took advantage of the free time and came to my house. It seemed we saw too little of each other those days and I was delighted when she stopped by. But my delight turned to disbelief when she told me her news.

"Jill, stop kidding around!" I snapped at my best friend. I was used to Jill's sense of humor, but that time she'd gone too far.

"I'm not kidding, Eva!" she insisted as she sat at the kitchen table sipping a glass of iced tea. "I asked my cousin, Tom, who's a lawyer. I wanted to be sure about this before I came over and told you. And Tom says it's true!"

I dropped onto the chair across from her. I wasn't sure how to react. Should I be glad? Sad? Angry? I wondered. All I knew was that I was confused. "How did you find out about this?"

"There was a news item on TV about a justice of the peace in the next state who performed fraudulent marriage ceremonies."

"If he's a justice of the peace, then any marriages he performs are legal," I argued. "That means that you and Kenny are married, and it means that Drew and I are married, too."

"Wrong." Jill leaned back in her chair. "I don't understand all of the legal stuff, but the man who performed our ceremonies wasn't really a justice of the peace. Therefore, he had no authority to perform weddings. Therefore, any weddings he did perform are invalid."

"Did you tell Kenny about this?" I asked. "What did he say about it?"

"Not yet. As soon as he gets home from work, I'll tell him. But I already know what he'll say. He'll say 'Let's get married all over again.' And then we will. Actually, I think it's sort of romantic—I get to marry my husband all over again!"

I sat listening to her chatter on about how soon they'd get married for real, what she would wear, and how maybe they'd even take a short honeymoon to make up for the one they never got to go on the first time.

Finally, she left and I was alone in my empty house. My mind was reeling from the impact of what Jill had told me. Drew and I weren't legally married! My mind couldn't even grasp the idea. What will Drew say when I tell him? Will he be glad? Will he be upset? Will he consider it an easy way out of a relationship that no longer truly exists? How do I feel about this situation? I asked myself.

Slowly, I walked into the living room, dropped onto the sofa, and picked up that framed photo of us again. I looked at our faces. Drew looked so young, happy, handsome, and eager for life. Me, I looked a little shy, but I also looked very happy as I stood close to the man I'd just married. A photo taken of us now would show tense shoulders and eyes clouded with weariness, anger, and unhappiness.

I was so weary of the nothingness of our relationship. Where is the love? Where is the spontaneity? Where are the moments of laughter and quiet tenderness and sweet passion?

What happened to those two people in that photograph? What happened to Drew and me? And more importantly, what's going to happen to us now?

Once more, I looked at the photograph and suddenly I recognized it for what it was—a LIE! The happiness it portrayed wasn't real just like our marriage wasn't real! At that moment, something inside of me snapped and I hurled the photo across the room and watched it smash against the wall.

That was the instant when Drew came into the room. "What's wrong?" he yelled as he raced toward me. "Are you alright? Why did you throw that picture?"

I hadn't heard him come in the back door. He was standing in front of me, demanding an explanation. I just sat there on the couch, too stunned by my own actions to even respond to him. I wanted to cry, but I couldn't. He reached out to touch me, and at the feel of his hands on my shoulders I started to sob. I wanted him to touch me; I needed him to touch me. But he had no right to touch me! He wasn't my husband!

A part of me was glad about that. I didn't want Drew to be my husband anymore. I wanted out of there and out of our wretched, lonely marriage. And then it dawned on me that I was, indeed, out of the marriage. In fact, I'd never truly been in the marriage! I didn't know whether to laugh or to cry, so I did both at the same time.

Evidently I became hysterical. That never happened before, so I had no idea what was going on with me or what was wrong with me. The world was whirling around me. Suddenly, Drew was standing over me. He pulled me into his arms, but I angrily shoved him away, picked up a cushion off the couch, and pitched it across the room. I watched it slap against the screen of the TV set and land on the floor.

I don't remember much of what happened next. I recall hearing Drew talking on the phone with Dr. Coyle. He found the bottle of pills in my purse and insisted that I take one. He made me a cup of tea and sat beside me on the couch while I sipped it.

Somehow, I managed to explain to him that our marriage was not a marriage. I went on to add that our house was not a home and that I didn't love him—never had and never would—because I loved him. I knew I was making no sense with my rambling words, but it didn't matter because nothing mattered. Besides, I knew that in a few minutes he'd have to go back to the warehouse and work for Phil. He always had to go back to work.

That night was a turning point for us. My hysteria acted as a catalyst and brought out into the open all of the anger and frustration that had been festering inside for so long. It also made Drew realize how entrenched he'd become in his work at the warehouse. He loves his job and he's very good at what he does. He's an achiever—perhaps an overachiever. Those are traits I admired in him even before we were married. He'd earned every promotion that Phil had given him, but the price he paid was too high. Every moment of every day was devoted to Phil. Every decision was balanced against what would please Phil the most. It was almost as though Drew was married to his job instead of to me.

Well, technically, he wasn't married to me at all and that put everything in a new perspective. That meant that Drew was free to do whatever he wanted to do and be with whoever he wanted to be with. And I was sure that he really wanted to be with Peggy—the perfect, beautiful, office manager who, like Drew, was determined to climb to the top of the corporate ladder. At the thought of Peggy I started to sob again because I knew that he'd leave me and go to her.

When Drew realized what I was thinking, he knelt in front of me, placed a hand on either side of my face, and forced me to look directly at him. Through my own tears, I saw the anguish on his face and the tears begin to stream down his cheeks.

"You think I want to be with Peggy?" he asked, surprised. "Are you serious, Eva?"

"Of course I am."

"Eva, that could never happen. I work with Peggy every day and she's a great office manager, but I'd never want to be with her! After all, she and her husband are back together and they are expecting a child." Then he added with a chuckle, "I can't picture her being a mother, but she's going to be one and she's very excited about it."

Drew and I sat up half the night talking. It was the first time we'd truly communicated in a long time. We discussed all of the things that had been affecting us, influencing us, and impacting our relationship.

I told him that I didn't like his drinking. It frightened me when he stayed out drinking at Frankie G's with his pals and then drove home. If he wasn't safe at home with me, I'd be afraid every time I heard a siren during the night. He promised me that he would stop drinking. He, too, realized that he was using it as a crutch to help him deal with the fact that so often he had too much to do and too many demands from Phil. He felt overwhelmed.

He also realized that he'd let his job become the focal point of his life. His job is important to him, but I'm important, too. He promised to find a way to balance the two and keep things in proper perspective.

Drew and I realized that there were serious problems in our relationship, and at Dr. Coyle's suggestion we began seeing a counselor. Dr. Larrimore helped us both come to terms with the stresses that nearly destroyed our marriage. He helped us to see that even though we got married too young, we did that because we truly love each other. And after facing the trauma of almost losing each other, we have gained a new, deeper love—one that we know will last a lifetime.

I used to think that the happiest day of my life was when I married Drew in front of a justice of the peace in that small town across the state line. But, in truth, the most incredible day of my life was when Drew and I exchanged marriage vows in a quiet ceremony in the chapel of the church we attend. Of course, all of Drew's family was there. Pa Hanson walked me down the aisle, Dina was my bridesmaid, and Ma Hanson and Mom—and even little Eric—stood right there beside me as I once again became Mrs. Andrew Hanson.

My life has changed a lot since my second wedding day. Drew still works too much, but not nearly as much as he used to and he no longer relies on alcohol to help him calm down after a busy day. He now prefers to relax at home with me and our son, Ryan. Though I'm not sure that trying to keep up with a two-year-old is exactly relaxing! I work part-time at the library, and while I'm there Mom watches Ryan for me. She loves being a doting grandmother.

Last night, I saw another shooting star and I wished that the happiness I have now would last forever.

THE END

OUR SECOND TIME AROUND

Romance filled the air with its sweetness and gave wings to any sadness I may have felt about my daughter leaving home. Rory was getting married in two months. She was so much in love and so full of joy, you could almost hear a choir of angels sing when she was around. Tim, her fiancé, was a great guy, and I was happy for them.

As I prepared dinner, an image of my beautiful daughter in her wedding gown filled my thoughts. Then, I heard her voice as she came through the door. "Mom, Daddy called me at work today." She planted a kiss on my cheek and added, "He wanted to know if you were taking someone to the wedding, or if he would have the honor of escorting you."

I was stunned that my ex-husband had asked about me. The situation had troubled me since we began planning the wedding. I closed my eyes. A warm rush ran through my entire body at just the thought of Ryan.

"What did you tell him?" I asked, trying to stay composed.

"I told him I thought you were going alone and that I would like very much for the two of you to go together." Rory's eyes met mine with a pleading look.

Taking a deep breath, I asked, "Do you think he really wants to go with me?"

Rory nodded and answered, "Daddy said he would love to go with you—provided you were agreeable."

I smiled and said, "Sure, I'd be delighted to."

My daughter wrapped her arms around me. "Thanks, Mom. Dad said he'd call me in the morning for your answer. He's away on an assignment right now."

Changing the subject, I quipped, "Let's get dinner on the table. You know your brother is always on the brink of fainting from hunger when he comes home."

Moments later, Todd strutted into the kitchen. "I'm starved. Is dinner ready?"

"It will be by the time you wash up." Rory and I exchanged a smile.

Todd had a landscaping job over the summer; in spite of his six-foot frame, he looked like a little boy coming in from playing in the mud. It didn't seem possible that he would be going back to college in two weeks.

Immediately after asking the blessing on our meal, Rory told her brother about their dad and me being together for the wedding.

Todd's eyes opened wide as a smile spread across his face. He even stopped shoveling food into his mouth long enough to speak. "That's great, Mom. When I was at Matthew's wedding, his parents both showed up with a date and it created a lot of tension. It'll be much nicer than going alone. Pass the potatoes," he added without missing a beat.

"You make some good points," I conceded as I handed him the bowl. "And it'll be nice to see your father after all these years."

With a dreamy look in her eyes, Rory said, "It's exciting to think of you and Dad together again—even if it is only for one day."

"I'm very surprised there isn't someone special in your dad's life; someone else, maybe, who he'd want to bring."

"Funny, Dad said the same about you," Rory responded.

The kids had remained close to their dad and spent a lot of time with him, but they never mentioned him having a girlfriend. Though it was tempting, I never pumped them for information. Knowing Ryan's passionate nature, I'd figured there had to be some women in his life. The thought hurt me deeply, even though we'd been divorced for ten years.

Every summer, Ryan's entire family would rent cottages on the beach and have a two-week reunion. That allowed our kids to stay close to his family, as well. Even when he had them on the alternating holiday schedules, his extended family was always around.

Throughout the rest of the meal I couldn't keep my mind off of Ryan. The thought of seeing him and that he would be by my side at the wedding brought alive so many feelings I'd tried to deny for years. I was shaking inside and tears swelled in my eyes, but I blotted them away before they were noticed.

Both the kids had plans for after dinner. I was glad to have the time alone for a good cry to release my emotions and to reflect.

Ryan and I had reached a point where we needed different things and couldn't share a life together anymore. After the divorce we had very little contact. I still loved him, and even the sound of his voice on the phone was painful. We spoke only on matters concerning the children, and that was usually in regard to making travel arrangements to see him.

The children were only thirteen and eleven when we divorced, but they'd experienced plenty of travel at a very early age.

It had been the constant relocating that Ryan's military career demanded that had destroyed our happiness. The depression I sank into was like a pool of quicksand, each move sucking me down even deeper. I needed a stable life—the kind of life Ryan and I vowed we would have when we got married.

When the children began developing emotional problems because of the constant upheaval in their lives, I couldn't put up a front any longer. I wanted to save them from the pain that Ryan and I suffered growing up in military families. I feared the love we shared—as a family—would turn to resentment and hatred.

Ryan's family had a long line of military men, whereas my dad was the only one in my family who was in the military.

We met when both our fathers were stationed in Texas. His family had been there about a year when mine arrived. We were both sixteen. The memory of the first time I saw him lived vividly in my heart.

I was the first one to arrive for English class. Watching the kids come into the room, laughing and talking, it was easy to pick out the ones that had been friends for years. The closest thing I had to friends like that were the kids in my maternal grandparent's neighborhood. Gram and Pop lived in a small town in Pennsylvania, and my younger brother, John, and I spent a month there every summer. Feeling miserable about all the friendships my father's career had ended, I vowed not to bother making any friends at my new school. I was sick of being the perpetual "new kid."

Then I saw Ryan. He was the last one through the door. Even from a distance I could see the sparkle in his big, gorgeous eyes—definitely kind eyes. He looked so sexy in his tight jeans. Suddenly, I was beginning to like it there.

Listening carefully as the teacher called roll, I watched to see what name he responded to. Ryan Brennan was the name I waited to hear. I was so captivated with him, I didn't hear Mrs. McKenna call my name. I came back to reality hearing, "For the third time— is Gina Falco in the classroom?"

Embarrassed, I meekly responded, "Present."

I tried to think of a way to meet Ryan without appearing brazen. I began arriving at school early and sitting on a bench at the main entrance. Ryan seemed to be popular; as soon as he set foot on campus, he'd be surrounded by kids. I'd peek over the book I pretended to be reading, and sometimes, it looked like he was checking me out.

Then one morning, after a week or so, I found Ryan sitting on the bench. My mouth hung open with surprise as my heart did flip-flops. He looked up from his notebook and asked, "Hi, I know you usually sit here and read. Would you mind sharing the bench with me?"

I felt my smile blossom from ear to ear as I answered, "I'd love to have the company." Sitting down beside him, I said, "I think we have the same English class—I'm Gina."

"Yeah, we do. I've noticed you around. I'm Ryan Brennan." Putting his books on the other side of him, he moved a little closer and took mine and added them to the pile. I could feel my body tingle in places it never had before. I didn't know what was happening to me, but it was exciting.

As the kids walked by and greeted him, he just said hello and stayed with me. When it was time to go to class, he picked up all the books and asked, "Is it okay if I walk you to your homeroom?"

Two weeks later he asked me to the movies. We sat in the back row kissing throughout most of the show. The following Monday morning he seemed nervous when I joined him on our bench. "Is something wrong?" I asked.

He swallowed hard as he reached into his pocket. It was a friendship ring!

Nervously, he asked, "Gina, will you be my steady girl?"

"Oh, yes!" I could feel my insides shaking as I threw my arms around his neck and we kissed. Remembering where we were, we unwillingly pulled apart and pretended to be interested in our homework assignments.

Almost immediately, we started planning a life together. It was our hope that neither of our fathers would get orders for a new duty station before we graduated. Ryan was on the football team and we had lots of friends. We were both happy and wanted things to stay the same until we had control over our own lives. Yet we knew the Army controlled our lives, and that haunted us.

"I never want a life that has anything to do with the military. I want my children to have a place to call home—with permanent friends," I said to Ryan.

"I know what you mean, Gina. It hurts to make friends only to lose them in nine months or a year or two." He kissed me and said, "I want a stable life for my family, too."

I continued to share my dreams with him. "I always wished I could live in the little town in Pennsylvania where my mother's parents live. I have relatives there, and friends I've known all my life from visiting my grandparents."

"Gina, if there is any possible way, we'll live in that town after we're married." His words warmed my heart and made me love him even more.

When school let out for the summer, my family took our

yearly trip to Gram's and Pop's. As usual, John and I stayed on for a couple more weeks after Mom and Dad left. I missed Ryan terribly and wished he could be there to share the joy I felt in that small town.

It was the middle of July when John and I returned to Texas. I called Ryan the moment I got home. He borrowed the car and we rode out to a secluded place in the nearby park. It felt so good to see him and feel his arms around me.

"Ryan, I missed you something awful." Our kisses became even more intense.

"Gina, I never want to be away from you so long again. I love you so very much."

"I love you, too, Ryan."

For the first time, our necking graduated to petting, but we didn't go any further. A part of me wanted to—but I was still shy and not ready to take that step.

It was four weeks later when the news came that we dreaded. Ryan's dad received orders for California. We were devastated at the thought of being torn apart. It all seemed so unfair. We were both going to be seniors, and Ryan had a starting position on the football team. He asked if he could stay behind with my family or one of his friends. The coach even offered Ryan a place. But his parents wanted their family together.

Ryan and I spent every possible moment together. The town had its Heritage Festival his last weekend there. It was a carnival atmosphere with games, rides, crafters, dancing, and all kinds of fun things. But I couldn't enjoy it. All I wanted to do was cry.

As we walked around holding hands, I stopped and looked into his eyes and said, "I really want to be alone with you. I'll get the stuff together for a picnic. I want to go somewhere."

"If I can get the car, we can drive to Sugar Bush Creek by the waterfall."

"That's a wonderful idea!" I said. "It's so pretty there."

With everyone at the festival, the place was deserted. We spread our blanket under the shade of the trees. As I was straightening out my side of the blanket, I felt something in my sandal crawling between my toes. I threw myself on the blanket, kicking and yelling, "Get it out! Quick! Get it out!"

Ryan came over and was trying to catch my foot. "Hold still. I can't get a hold of it!" Finally, he was able to remove my sandal. He flung the creeping creature in the woods. With my dilemma solved, we both started to laugh. Then we became aware of his hand on my leg. Our eyes locked in a gaze that I felt deep in my soul. He ran his hand up my leg and rolled over on me.

Our lips met in a tender kiss, and he let them trail down my neck. When his lips returned to mine, our kisses became long, hard, and passionate.

Unable to deny our desire, Ryan and I claimed each other's virginity. As we lay together, enjoying the beauty of the experience, I felt new and discovered.

From that time on, Ryan and I took every possible opportunity to make love. It was early the following Saturday that his family left. When we said good-bye, he took me in his arms. "As soon as I graduate, I'll come for you and we'll get married. In the meantime, I'll write you every day." I couldn't speak through the tears that choked me. It felt like my heart was being ripped from my body.

Consumed with grief, I cried all of the time. Mom tried being supportive by saying things like, "Honey, if it's meant to be, your love for each other will be there in a year. School is starting next week and once you're back with your friends and activities, it'll be easier."

I knew she had no idea how deeply in love I was. I had no appetite and did a lot of throwing up. After a few weeks, Mom asked, "Gina, do you think you should see a doctor?"

I wailed back, "What can a doctor do for a broken heart? I hate the military!" I continued to rant as I went into my room and slammed the door.

One morning, about a month later, Mom said to me, "Gina, you're not going to school today. I think there's something physically wrong with you. I've made you a doctor's appointment."

"There's nothing physically wrong with me," I protested.

"I would feel better if you had a check-up. No more arguing; get in the car."

My examination revealed I was pregnant. When Dr. Morris told me the news, I cried like my heart was breaking. Mom put her arms around me and said, "We'll get through this, Gina." Her voice cracked as she tried to hold back tears.

As we drove home I kept saying, "I'm so sorry." Then I asked, "What will Daddy say?"

"We'll talk about it when he comes home. Now try to calm down."

When we got home, Mom and I hugged each other and cried for a long time. "Today has been a shock for you. Why don't you lay down until dinner is ready?" Mom said.

I fell asleep and woke up around seven-thirty. I crossed the hall to the bathroom. When I came out, Mom and Dad were waiting for me. Mom offered me dinner, but I wasn't hungry. "Then I think we need to talk," Dad said.

We went to my room. I sat on my bed with my head down, sobbing. "I'm sorry I let you down. I must be a big disappointment."

Dad said, "Never mind about us. You, Ryan, and the baby are the ones we need to be concerned about."

I could tell by his voice that he was trying not to show his emotions. He put his hands on my shoulders and said, "Gina, the first thing you need to do is tell Ryan. Then think about if you want to keep the baby. Your mother and I could raise the child, or you could give it up for adoption, or—" Dad stopped as he searched for the right words to use, then he added, "Or the other alternative."

Tears were in his eyes. "Oh, Daddy, I don't think I could do that!" I started to cry and he pulled me in his arms.

"I just want you to be aware of all the options. Your mother and I love you and we will help you through this."

"Do you feel like calling Ryan now?" Mom asked.

"Yes, I really need to talk to him."

I wondered what his reaction would be. I made several attempts at dialing his number before I completed it. Would he be mad? Might he say it was my problem, like a lot of boys did? My heart was racing; when I heard Ryan speak I started to cry.

"Gina, what's wrong?" His voice was urgent as he repeated the question until I could get the words out.

"Ryan, I . . . I'm pregnant."

He said nothing for a while, and the silence seemed to last an eternity. Then he said, "Gina, I'm sorry. This is my fault. But it's not a problem—it's a solution. Now we can be married. You know that was my plan right after graduation. I love you. Will you marry me?"

Without hesitation, I answered, "Yes! Ryan, I want to be with you for the rest of my life, and I love you with all my heart."

"I'm going to take the best care I possibly can of you and our baby. I guess the first thing I have to do is tell my parents. I'll call you back—love you."

"Love you, too."

Ryan made me feel so wonderful. From that moment, he was my hero—my knight in shining armor—taking me to his kingdom to live happily ever after.

I told my parents the news. "Ryan and I want to get married!" When they didn't respond right away, I realized with both of us being seventeen we may possibly need our parents to sign something. I added, "Is that okay with you? He's telling his parents now; he'll call me back tonight."

They looked at each other, then Dad said, "We thought that might be the case. When he calls back we'll need to talk to his parents and hear how they feel about it."

"While we're waiting for Ryan's call, you should eat, Gina. You've eaten nothing all day." Mom went to the kitchen and returned with a bowl of soup. I could feel her shaking as she handed it to me. As I ate, Mom and Dad talked about the responsibilities of marriage and parenthood, and how young we were to be dealing with them.

I couldn't believe how calm they were. I looked at them and said, "I'm sorry I hurt you. Thank you for being so wonderful and not screaming and yelling."

Mom smiled. "We suspected it when you started to display the classic symptoms. So, it wasn't a shock to us."

Dad put his arm around me. "Yelling and screaming wouldn't help or change a thing."

Ryan called back in about an hour. "How'd your parents take the news?" I asked.

"Right now, they're pretty upset. I told them we want to get married, and I think that worries them."

As we talked, it sounded like Ryan's parents had the same talk about responsibility that mine had. I could hear voices in the background, then Ryan said, "Gina, my parents want to talk to your parents."

"Mine are waiting to speak with yours, also."

Our parents talked for a long time. Afterward, they told me what they had decided.

"Gina, we all agreed the two of you are very young for marriage." Dad stopped and cleared his throat. "But we feel you and Ryan are sincere and deeply committed to each other." His voice began to fade.

Mom picked up the conversation as she nervously twisted a tissue. "We want you and Ryan to take two weeks to make a decision—or longer if you need it. Go to school and think about what you will be missing. If you still want to get married, then you will have our blessing."

Dad rubbed his eyes and continued, "However, we think it best you and Ryan have no contact during this time. Just concentrate on what you will have to give up."

"This is the rest of you life we're talking about." Mom squeezed my hand. "We don't want you and Ryan to resent each other, or the baby someday."

I thought it was the least I could do to honor my parents. I agreed to their terms.

I never realized how much fun there was being a teenager until I had to think about giving it up. No more football games or trips to the mall just for fun. However, with Dad's military career, new orders could come any day, ending the friendships I had made at school. Above all else, my heart ached for Ryan.

At the end of the two weeks I told my parents I still wanted to marry Ryan.

Dad sighed heavily. "You're sure this is what you want?"

"Yes. I gave it a lot of thought, and it is what I want."

When I saw a tear trickle down Mom's cheek, I started to cry and hugged her. She tucked a stray hair behind my ear and patted my back. "I guess you need to make a phone call."

As I dialed Ryan's number, the thought occurred to me—what if Ryan no longer wanted to get married? I started to shake, and then I heard his voice.

"Hi, it's me." My lips were moving but I couldn't get words to come out.

"Gina, my parents and I just finished talking and I was going to call you."

There was an awkward silence. It seemed we were both waiting for the other to give their decision first. Finally, Ryan asked, "Gina, do you still want to get married?"

"Yes, if you do."

"I do—very much. I love you, Gina."

"I love you, too. I'm so happy!"

There were many phone calls as our plans were being made. Since I didn't want to go school once I started to show and the baby would be born before graduation, it was decided I'd go to California. Since his dad was just transferred, it was very likely he could finish his education without interruptions. Ryan and I would be married and live with his parents until he graduated and got a job.

With our wedding only three weeks away, I dropped out of school and used the time to go through my things. One Saturday, I was out in the garage looking through some of the boxes that followed us around but never got unpacked before we had to move again. I came across my fielder's glove and ball cap and got a little misty.

One of Dad's longest assignments was three years in Kentucky. I was on a girls' softball team and was chosen for the league all-star team the last year I was there. It was a dream come true for me. The day after I was picked, Dad got orders and we left quickly, so that John and I could start the school year at the new place. I was twelve and moving for the fifth time. That one was the most painful and caused me to hate military life.

I put the hat on and slipped my hand into the glove. I started punching the pocket when Dad walked in behind me. "You played really good ball. You deserved to be on that all-star team." He put his arm around me. "Sorry my orders messed things up for you."

"It's okay, Dad. You had no control over it—it wasn't your fault."

That night I went to John's room and handed him the glove. "Would you like to have this? Don't think I'll be needing it."

"Yeah, it's a great glove. Thanks!" His eyes brimmed with tears. "I'm going to miss you, Gina. You're my best friend as well as my sister."

I started to cry and we hugged. "I'll miss you, too. Take care of yourself—your big sister won't be around to watch out for you anymore."

That night it hit me hard—I was leaving my family and how much I loved them. Suddenly, I was frightened by the plans I'd made. I lay in bed sobbing like a little girl. A soft knock came at my door. "Gina, it's Mom; can I come in?"

I blotted my eyes with my blanket and whimpered, "Sure."

She sat on the edge of my bed and cuddled me like she had when I was little. It was so comforting and I felt so secure. "Mom, I'm scared about leaving you and Dad."

"We'll always be here for you. I know the future can be frightening—no one ever knows what lies ahead. Daddy and I are proud of how you and Ryan are handling your responsibility. All you can do is try your best." She kissed my forehead. "Can I tell you a love story?"

Baffled by her request, I just nodded.

"About eighteen years ago a young girl in Pennsylvania was about to start college. That summer she worked as a waitress in her hometown. There was an Army post about fifteen miles away. The soldiers were in town working on a project to flood a valley and create a man-made lake. The restaurant she worked at was close to the project and a lot of the soldiers ate there. The girl was strongly attracted to one of them and he liked her, too."

"Mom, do I know these people?"

"See if you can figure it out."

She continued, "They started to see each other and fell madly in love. She was wishing she didn't have to go away to college, even though it was only sixty miles away. He promised to come see her every chance he could and she vowed to get home as often as possible. Then he was being sent far away and it seemed like the end of their world. He wanted to marry her and take her with him.

66

But she said she had to finish the semester because her parents paid for it and they didn't have money to waste. They were in love, and desperate. Anytime they could, they met and made love. When he left for Alaska, she was pregnant."

"Mom, I was born in Alaska. You mean you and Dad had to get married?"

She smiled. "Not had to—wanted to. I was eighteen and Dad was nineteen. I was young and scared, too. The point is, we understand what you are going through. I think you know Dad and I have been very happy. Maybe that will give you some confidence."

"Thanks for sharing your love story with me. I feel much better."

That night, it was like Mom took me by the hand and walked me across the bridge from childhood to womanhood. I saw her as a woman and a friend as well as a mother.

The remaining days passed quickly. My parents and John flew to California to attend the wedding. It was small; besides my family, there was Ryan's parents and his two older brothers.

At first I was uncomfortable during the day, alone with Ryan's mother. But she was good to me. Occasionally, she'd say, "I always wanted a daughter." She showed me how to make Ryan's favorite dishes.

Our daughter, Rory, was born a month before Ryan graduated. He glowed every time he looked at her. One night he snuggled her little body against his heart, saying, "She is so tiny and helpless. I can't believe how much I love her already. I want to be a good father and protect her and provide for her the best I can."

Ryan was so sweet. I kissed him and said, "Rory already feels secure in your arms. She knows you love her and she loves you, too."

However, it wasn't long before reality set in. Ryan couldn't find a job that paid more than minimum. He took one with a promise of a raise in three months. But when the time came he was told it wasn't in the budget. He was upset that we couldn't afford a place of our own.

"Maybe I can get something part-time. I hear the servers at the Lamont make excellent tips. You and your mom can watch the baby a few nights a week."

"If we move out, it wouldn't be convenient for Mom to watch her. Since there are days I have to work overtime, our schedules may conflict. But you did give me an idea—I'm going to see if they're hiring full-time."

Ryan got hired and we moved into a tiny, run-down apartment.

To help make ends meet, I watched a little boy three days a week. But his tips were inconsistent; some weeks they were great and other times lousy. We were having problems meeting out expenses.

We frequently went to Ryan's parents' house for Sunday dinner. One evening when we came home, Ryan said, "Dad asked how things were going. I told him not as well as I would like." He paused a moment and nervously cleared his throat. "He suggested I go into the service and get some training."

"No!" I shouted. "You know I hate military life! I thought you did, too. Remember what you said when we were in Texas?"

Ryan grabbed hold of me. "Gina, calm down. Please listen to what I have to say."

I took a deep breath. "Okay."

"Dad said besides the training, if I enlist for three years I'll be twenty-one when I get out. Better jobs might be available to me when I'm a little older."

Pacing the floor, I asked, "What about Rory? I don't want her constantly changing schools, and I don't want to be a military wife!"

Ryan followed me around trying to take hold of me. I kept pushing him away. "Gina, Rory will only be four years old when I'm out. She won't even be in kindergarten. I want to provide better than this for our family. Please think about it."

I didn't talk to Ryan for a few days. I figured we'd only argue. But I thought about how we were living and realized he was actually making a sacrifice for Rory and me. I agreed as long as three years would be the end of it.

So, Ryan joined the Army. I stayed with my family until he was finished with his basic training and his job training. It was four months before Rory and I could join him. We missed each other terribly. When I got to him we ravished each other, making love every night—usually two or three times. It wasn't long before I became pregnant. Rory was two when Todd was born.

The day we came home from the hospital, Ryan held him in his arms. He began planning all the father-and-son things they would do together. He kissed me and said, "Thank you for my son, Gina. It's great having a daughter as beautiful as her mommy, and a son makes our family complete. It's going to be lots of fun buying toys!"

Todd had some intestinal problems and required a lot of medical care. There was a possibility he'd need surgery, but that would be determined when he was a little older.

Motherhood kept me busy, and I enjoyed it. We had moved twice and that also kept me busy. Ryan had been promoted and we were excited about the pay increase. The remainder of his enlistment went pretty fast, but I was still glad it was over.

We were in Florida when Ryan was discharged. His computer training even got him a decent job. But he wasn't eligible for benefits until his six-month probation period was up. That proved to be disastrous for us. Todd needed the surgery and we couldn't possibly pay for it.

Knowing how ill our little son was made us terribly sad. We held him constantly, even while he slept. We prayed he wouldn't be taken from us.

"Gina, we need to talk about Todd's surgery. The problem is I make a little too much to qualify for assistance. The doctor and hospital bills will be tremendous; it will take years for us to pay them off."

"I was thinking of getting a job—we could use my income to pay the medical bills," I said.

Ryan ran his fingers through his hair. "Would there be enough left after we pay child care for two children? Besides, Todd will need special care for a while, and I think no one would care as much as us. He'll need his mother."

"I don't know what else to do, Ryan." I blotted away my tears and looked into his eyes. "We'll pay the bills the rest of our lives if we need to."

Ryan took hold of my hand and kissed it. "There is another option. I could go back in the Army."

"I don't want that!" I shouted and pulled my hand from his.

"Gina, please listen. It's the most logical solution. When I was discharged they said if I re-enlisted in three months I would lose no rank or pay." He put his head in his hands. "You know all the medical care will be provided by the Army. The most important thing is our son's health. The three months are almost up, and I have to act fast."

I began to cry. As much as I hated the service, it did seem to be the best answer to our problem. "You're right, Ryan. Todd's health is the most important thing—my dreams can wait. But, please, this has to be the last time."

Ryan went back for another three years. Todd had his surgery, and fortunately, it was a success. Our hearts were filled with joy and gratitude for the healthy, normal life it gave him.

We moved twice during those years. When Ryan got down to two months to go, I began to feel free to plan a civilian life. I looked forward to buying a home and never moving again. Rory was six and Todd four; I wanted them in a school district where they would stay until they graduated and not be the constant new kids. Ryan had gotten another promotion and I did some baby-sitting. We managed to save a little money, and I was ready to make the transition to the life I'd always wanted.

I noticed for a few days that when I'd want to talk about the future, Ryan would get evasive. I kissed him and asked, "Is something wrong? You don't seem to be interested in making plans."

He held me in his arms and said, "Gina, we need to talk."

I felt a shiver go up my spine, and it seemed to take forever for Ryan to get the words out. "Gina, first I want you to know you and the children are the most important things in the world to me." I felt my knees shake when he paused. "I'm having second thoughts about leaving the service."

"You can't be serious!" I sat down at the kitchen table, put my face in my hands, and cried. "Why would you even consider this? You've known since high school I never wanted a military life again!"

Ryan pulled a chair up next to me, took my hands from my face, and said, "Please hear me out. My commanding officer told me I've been selected for Officer's Training School if I stay in the Army." Ryan tried to kiss me but I turned away. "Gina, you know that's a great honor . . . and it will mean a big advancement for me in rank and also in pay. As we both know, civilian life can be a rat race when it comes to employment. Our futures will be secure. I will have to re-enlist for six years."

I got up and started pacing. "Ryan, what about the vows we made in Texas? That we were never going to drag our children all over the place like we'd been!" When he tried to take hold of me, I pounded his chest. "Have you considered my feelings? Please don't do this to me and the kids!"

Ryan handed me his handkerchief and pulled me to him. "If I leave now, I lose a great opportunity. But if I leave the service as an officer, it should help me get a better job. Otherwise, I'll probably have to work days and go to college at night to get anywhere."

Over the next several days, I calmed down and thought more open-mindedly about what Ryan had said. I understood his fears and realized his strong sense of responsibility. Little did I know that sense of responsibility would be a contributor to the end of our marriage.

Finally, I went to my husband and said, "I love you and appreciate how much you care about the children and me. If I hadn't had gotten pregnant, you probably would have gone on to college, maybe even on a football scholarship. And you wouldn't have had to go into the service." I nervously wrung my hands as memories of my gypsy childhood flashed through my mind. "Just remember—I can't spend the rest of my life as a military wife. But I can try to give it a few more years."

"Thank you, Gina." He kissed me, and then added, "Please don't ever think I resent you because you got pregnant. After all, I was responsible, too. I've never regretted our marriage or our little girl."

We kissed, and soon we were making love for the first time in days. It felt good to be close again.

When Ryan graduated, I was so proud of him that I almost thought I could adjust. But only weeks after the ceremony, he got new orders. I'd spent my entire life packing and unpacking, trying to decide what to do about cozy winter clothes that wouldn't be needed at the new location, or the opposite situation. Do I hold on to them in case we'll need them at next duty station? Will the kids outgrow theirs before they need them again? Should we just sell our furnishings and avoid the hassle of moving them? Tears gushed down my face. I sat on the floor and cried for hours. I went into a depression.

Over the next two years I tried hard not to get close to anyone. I'd become one of the things I hated most as a kid—the kind of military wife who was always gracious, but who lacked any true feelings. I felt so superficial and empty.

When Ryan's next orders came, I couldn't believe our good fortune. He was being sent to the base in Pennsylvania where my parents met. We were actually going to the place I thought of as home. Dad retired from the service and he and Mom settled there. John was married with three children and lived there, too. Plus, there was Mom's extended family and the friends I'd made during visits to my grandparents.

"Ryan, I'm so happy! I didn't think this would ever happen." I read the papers repeatedly to make sure we weren't missing something.

He smiled and pulled me in his arms. "I didn't want to say anything in case it didn't come through, but I requested that base. As you know, a request really doesn't mean much. They send you where they feel you're needed. But this time, it worked out!"

"Thank you, Ryan." I cried tears of joy.

Soon we were making love with more passion than we had for a long time. Afterward, Ryan held me in his arms. "It's great to see you so happy."

I was excited when we arrived and found an old Victorian home for sale near my parents. "Ryan, it's the kind of home I always wanted! And it has a great yard. Let's buy it—please!"

Ryan was leery, though. "Gina, you know I might get orders before the remainder of the six years are up. What if we have to leave?"

Tears stung my eyes; I put my arms around his neck. "Ryan, please do this for me. I've followed you all over the country. This is important to me. We'll cross that bridge when and if we come to it."

He smiled. "Okay, we'll do it."

We were all happy there. The kids loved having Gramps and Grammy nearby. And they had cousins to share their life as well as friends. One night, as we tucked Todd in, we overheard his prayers: "And thank You, God, for sending us here with all these people who love me." It brought tears to both our eyes.

The holidays were even more wonderful than I had imagined. Ryan's parents were able to come and stay for a week, making the family complete. It was the perfect life.

Come spring, Rory registered for softball and I signed up to help out. When the league president called to ask if I wanted to manage the team, I was thrilled. Ryan helped with coaching and we had loads of fun. Being involved with Rory's team helped to mend the break in my heart when Dad's orders ruined my all-star season so many years earlier.

Todd and my dad became the best of buddies. During the summer months they were up at the crack of dawn to go fishing. Even in the winter when the lake froze, they'd ice fish. Everything was going wonderfully for my family.

We were there for almost three years. I'd begun to think that since Ryan had only a year left he wouldn't get new orders. But that soon proved to be wrong. Late May, he was told he was being transferred to Oklahoma.

We held off telling the children. One reason was because we were arguing about the future. As we lay in bed one night, Ryan said, "Gina, time is running out; we have to tell the kids and make our plans. Maybe we can rent the house?"

I put my finger to his lips. "Ryan, what I'm about to say is very difficult." Pausing, I tried to find the right words. "It's only a year. I don't think we should uproot the children. It would be very hard on them. Remember how we used to feel about it?" Tears were pooling in my eyes. "I'm not going to join you."

His eyes widened. "Gina, I was afraid this would happen if we bought this house! You've gotten too attached!"

"Don't blame it on this house, Ryan! You know I never wanted to be a military wife. I promised to try, and I have. I can't do it anymore."

I got out of bed, hoping to walk off some of the tension. Ryan took me in his arms. "Gina, I love you and the kids. I need you with me. Keeping the family together is very important to me." I could see the tears he tried to hold back. "Maybe they'll be okay with it. Let's see how they feel."

So the next day, we told them. Ryan said, "Daddy has orders for Oklahoma—"

"No! I don't want to go anywhere!" Rory cried. "I have to stay here. The team needs me. And they need you, too, Mom." Rory went on with a list of reasons for staying, and at the end, added, "Besides that, I love it here."

Todd was also crying. "I won't be able to fish with Gramps anymore, or compete in the tournament! I'll never see my friends! Can I stay and live with Gramps and Grammy?"

"That's a good idea!" Rory piped up. "Can we?"

After listening to more of their pleas, Ryan took them in his arms. "Mommy and I will have to talk about this. We'll see if we can work something out."

"You're right; it would be hard on them. I guess I can go alone and come home when I have leave time. Will you bring them out to see me sometimes?" Ryan asked after the kids had left the room.

"Sure I will." We held onto each other, crying. "I'll miss you so much."

"I'll miss you and the kids, too."

The arrangement wasn't perfect, but it worked pretty well. We managed to spend a good deal of quality time together.

When Ryan came home for what was to be his last visit before being discharged, I thought he looked tense. "Is there something wrong?" I asked when we were finally alone.

"Gina, you know I love you deeply." He stepped back and turned away from me. Thoughts were spinning through my head as to what he might be trying to say. I wondered if he was going to confess to an affair.

"What is it, Ryan?" I went to him and he sat me down in a chair.

"Gina, you're not going to like what I have to say." His face was tight and his voice firm as he spoke slowly. "I'm sorry, but I can't leave the service."

"What do you mean you can't leave? You promised me." I started to shake and tears poured down my face. "Ryan, I can't be a military wife any longer. You must know that. Remember when we met and you said you didn't want this life, either?" I slammed my fist on the dresser.

"Please listen, and try to understand. When we met, I saw the world through the eyes of a kid. Now that I'm a man I see things differently." He kissed my forehead and continued, "The Army was there when I needed to support my family and when my son needed surgery. It honored me by making me an officer. There's a force inside I can't deny. I feel an obligation to serve my country and this organization."

"What about your obligation to me?" I lashed out.

"I still want to be a good husband and father. I want to be a good solider, too."

"Ryan, I have needs and desires I've been putting aside since we've been married. Don't they mean anything to you?" I searched his eyes for an answer before he began to speak.

"Of course, they do. Making you happy is very important to me, but being a soldier is the only thing I know how to do." Ryan pointed to the picture of his dad in uniform and said, "I guess I've followed in the footsteps of my dad, my grandfather, and his father. They've all made a career out of the military."

My head was ready to explode. For a moment, I hated Ryan, his dad, and anything to do with the military.

But he continued making his case. "Another thing, I have all these years in that will count toward retirement. We'll only be in our forties then, and we'll be able settle in one place."

I slumped onto the bed. "That's a long time for me to wait! The kids would have to change schools several times and they're so happy here. Have you actually re-enlisted already?"

"No, I wanted to tell you first."

"Ryan, I won't join you. I have the life I want here. That force that drives you to serve is the same one that makes a home sacred to me."

He lay down beside me. "Gina, I need you with me. Please come to me. I don't want a long-distance marriage."

I shrugged. "Maybe our marriage is dying."

For the rest of his visit, we'd argue—and then make love in vicious cycles. I loved him dearly but hated the life I had to live with him.

The children were upset with their dad's decision, and begged not to move from the place they loved dearly.

The day Ryan left I felt like a dagger had been pushed through my heart. Our beautiful love seemed to be breaking apart like waves on a rocky shore.

Ryan's next assignment was Japan, which meant if I didn't join him we'd never see each other. Struggling to make a decision, I went for a walk in the park one autumn morning. The sun had just burned off the fog and the dew on the grass shimmered like diamond dust. I looked around at the trees ablaze with the gold and bronze of fall. My eyes followed treetops to the hills beyond, where brilliantly colored leaves seemed to reach up and touch the sky. I could almost feel the hills wrap around me like giant arms pulling me close to a loving heart. The breeze seemed to whisper, "This is your home."

Would I ever be free of the conflict inside me? It seemed my heart wanted wings to go to the man I loved, but my soul had found its earthly home. I was hurt and angered by Ryan's decision. Every time we spoke on the phone it ended in an argument. Sick of the turmoil, I finally told him, "We no longer have a marriage. If we can't make a life together, then we should free each other. I want a divorce."

"I can't believe you want to end our marriage!" His words were broken as though punctured by tears.

"It's not you I want to divorce—it's the military. Don't you understand that?"

We argued for a while. In the end, Ryan said, "Do what you feel you have to. Just remember I never wanted the divorce."

I was disappointed. I'd hope he'd say he'd finish this tour of duty and leave the military. My heart was breaking, but I felt I had no choice but to start a life without Ryan.

The kids had a good life there. I got a part-time job and become active in community affairs. Several years after the divorce, I met a man. I liked him because he made me laugh, which made me feel comfortable with him. We started going out. When Doug wanted to become intimate, I thought maybe time was beginning to free me from my love for Ryan. But I was wrong. All it was for me was going through the motions of sex, and the only feeling I got out of it was embarrassment. It made me miss Ryan even more; I never dated again.

And now, there I was . . . thinking about being with Ryan at Rory's wedding.

Thoughts of Ryan with other women were driving me crazy, too. Since he brought up being with me at the wedding, it gave me hope that maybe there wasn't anyone special in his life.

The day of the rehearsal had arrived. I bought a new silk dress—a blue one. Ryan always loved the feel of silk, and blue was his favorite color. My daily exercise kept me in shape, and the silk clung to every curve of my body. I had highlights put in hair and even went for a makeup consultation. I liked the way I looked, and hoped Ryan would, too. No matter how hard I tried, I couldn't stop dreaming of Ryan and me together again.

As Rory, Todd, and I were leaving the house, Rory said, "Mom, you are absolutely beautiful."

Todd whistled and said, "She's right, Mom—you're a real looker!"

Rory said that Tim and his parents were already at the hotel and were waiting for his brothers and their families to arrive. She said they were all coming to the church together.

I was keeping a constant vigil on the door for Ryan. When I saw my ex-husband walk in and come toward me, I was mesmerized. He still had a thick head of hair; the few lines around his eyes only added character to his good looks. His beautiful eyes still sparkled. I wanted to say something but my brain couldn't make my mouth work. It was like that first day in Texas. Only this time, I knew why my body tingled in those places, and it was hard to ignore.

Ryan took hold of my hands and we just stared into each other's eyes for a while. "Gina, you look beautiful."

I could feel my blood rush through my body, but I had to stay cool. "Thank you, Ryan. You're as handsome as ever." Reaching to touch his shoulder, I added, "Looks like you've stayed in shape."

"Exercise got me through the lonely times." He kissed my cheek.

Rory and Todd came to greet their dad. Then Rory took him away to meet her future in-laws.

His words, "lonely times," kept going through my head. Could that mean he missed me?

At the rehearsal dinner Ryan and I sat across from each other. I couldn't keep my eyes off him. My body begged for his touch. I wanted to feel his lips pressed against mine. I hoped he was feeling what I was.

Alone in my bed that night, Ryan was all I could think about. Seeing him for those few hours made me aware of how much I still loved him. My bed never felt so empty. I wanted him there so much I swear I could feel his breath on my cheek. I wondered if his heart could feel mine reaching out to his.

The next day, when Ryan walked our daughter down the aisle, memories of her growing up and playing with her daddy ran through my mind like a home movie.

He took his place beside me in the pew. Tears kept creeping from my eyes as Rory and Tim exchanged their vows. Ryan turned toward me and I saw him blink away some tears. We shared a smile and he held my hand through the entire ceremony.

At the reception we managed to talk a little. He told me about the places he'd been and sometimes would say, "I think you would have liked it there."

I'd smiled and say, "I'm sure it would have been a lovely vacation for a few weeks." But I did tell him, "Sounds like you've had an exciting and interesting life."

Ryan went to the bar and came back with drinks for us. "What about you, Gina?" he asked, handing me my glass.

"I clerk part-time for the county. I deal with deeds and land records." Taking a sip of my wine, I continued, "It's how I started as volunteer in the historical society. Sometimes I'd have to research the deeds and would find so much fascinating information I wanted the community to know." Motioning toward the windows, I said, "If you noticed any of the gardens in town, I help with the garden society, too. Both mean a lot to me and I enjoy them tremendously."

As we danced, we talked about the kids. "They're both fine young people, Gina. You did a great job raising them. I wish I could have been with them more."

"I'm very happy with how they turned out. But I can't take all the credit. You've been a great father. Though you were far away they were close to you and knew how much you cared."

We stopped talking and he pulled me close. Our bodies rubbed together in slow, rhythmic moves. My desire for him was almost overwhelming.

When we returned to the table, I asked, "How long will you be in town?"

"Don't know right now. It depends on a certain matter." He smiled and said, "You know me, Gina—always have to do things in the proper order. Right now, first thing is Rory's wedding."

The night was over much too soon. I wanted to invite him back to our home for the night. But I knew he had to get his parents to the airport for an early flight. Besides, Todd and some out-of-town relatives were staying at the house. They intended to be on the road by eleven o'clock, which meant I'd be cooking breakfast early in the morning. But I was brokenhearted when Ryan didn't ask to see me again.

The next day, after Todd and the others had left, I felt so alone. I sat on the sofa holding a picture of the four of us and cried. Feeling the emptiness of the house, I wondered if it was worth the sacrifice of the man I loved.

I decided I couldn't let him go without trying to get him back. I jumped from the sofa, grabbed the phone directory, and started looking for the hotel where he was staying.

As I started dialing, I heard a knock at the door. When I opened it I couldn't believe my eyes. Ryan was standing there. He stepped in and I threw my arms around his neck. "Ryan, I was afraid I wouldn't see you before you left. I was just trying to call the hotel."

He held me tighter and we started to kiss. "Ryan, I love you and I'll go anywhere with you. I never want to be away from you."

"Gina, I came to tell you I'm retiring from the service. I love you and I'll live anywhere you want—as long as we're together."

Our kisses were passionate. He cupped my face with his hands. "I used to dream of you coming to me in the night, and when I'd reach out, you'd disappear," Ryan said.

I opened his shirt and slid my hands over the contours of his chest. To feel the beating of his heart and warmth of his flesh made me breathless.

Suddenly, he pulled back. Reaching in his pocket he brought out an engagement ring and slipped it on my finger. "I didn't have any money to buy one when we were married, but I hope this makes up for it. Gina, will you marry me—again?"

"Yes!" I kissed him. "In my heart, I never stopped being your wife. I had the house and the kids, but without you, it really wasn't a home."

Ryan carried me into the bedroom and we made love for hours. The magic was even more wonderful than before. As I lay snuggled in his arms, basking in the rapture of a sweet dream come true, I know I heard my own choir of angels sing.

THE END

ON THE BRINK OF DIVORCE
Our boys showed us how to love again

I could hear my nine-year-old twins quarrelling downstairs in the den. Since Paul had moved out, I noticed that they seemed to argue more.

This time it was over who would dominate the remote. When the noise level escalated again, I knew it was time to break the argument up. I finished folding the undershirt I'd started and went downstairs.

"Come on, guys. Enough is enough."

"He started it!" Michael declared.

"'Cause he's been hogging the remote and it's my turn to get it," Matthew whined.

"Uh-uh, I got it first."

"Look, guys. There's enough noise in here to break the sound barrier, not to mention my ears. If you two are incapable of sharing, I'll help out by sending you both to your rooms."

"No! Our show is coming on soon," Michael replied.

"Yeah. We can't miss it," Matthew added.

"So the problem is solved?"

"Yeah," both boys agreed.

I wished it were that easy to solve my own problems. Listening to my twins squabble reminded me of Paul and myself during the last months before our separation and his decision to take a promotion, moving him clear across the state. We seemed to argue about everything. Just like the boys, neither of us wanted to give in. I don't think we ever bothered to listen to ourselves. If we had, maybe we would've talked to one another instead of at one another and things might've turned out differently.

As I continued to fold the laundry, my mind began to wander. One particular morning suddenly came to mind. Paul had an important meeting to attend and had wanted me to wash and iron his blue dress shirt. Despite the fact I'd gotten up with a headache that morning, I forced myself to iron the shirt and hung it on a hanger, leaving it in the bedroom for him to find when he got out of the shower. Getting the kids finished with breakfast and off to school was my next priority. I didn't want them to be late again.

The boys had just gone out the front door to meet the school bus when I heard Paul calling me. I didn't find his tone of voice inviting.

I called up the steps, "What's wrong, Paul?" I caught myself before adding the word now.

"What's right?"

79

I sighed. This is going to be a fun morning, I thought as I reluctantly went upstairs to find out what his problem was.

Paul was standing in our bedroom, half dressed, holding the shirt I'd just ironed.

"You call this ironed?" he said, dangling the shirt inches from my nose.

"Would you prefer I used the term 'pressed'?"

"Cute, real cute."

I decided to get it over with and asked, "What's wrong with the shirt, Paul?"

"This is what's wrong with it," he said, pointing to a miniscule crease. "And this one and that one."

I thought he was being ridiculous. No one was going to see either crease under his jacket. "If you don't like the way I iron, you have recourse."

"I know. I can do it myself," he said, mimicking my voice.

"Or you can send it out to be laundered. This is America. You have the freedom to choose."

"I'm such a lucky man. I married a comedienne."

"And I married a perfectionist."

"What's wrong with that?"

"With a perfectionist, there's no room for improvement," I said, leaving him standing there as I went into the bathroom, slamming the door behind me.

My head was pounding a rhythm in time with my accelerated heartbeat. Why couldn't the man ever be happy? Why did he constantly have to nitpick? I popped two aspirin into my mouth and chased them down with a glass of water. Staring into the mirror at my bleary eyes, I hoped he'd finish dressing and leave so I could lie down in peace.

It occurred to me that most of our arguments were just as silly and petty as that one. The only ones that turned out to be serious concerned Paul's job. And those were dillies. We'd snip at one another for hours, never accomplishing anything more than being hurtful and mean.

I wondered if Paul might've applied for the new position so that he'd have a valid reason to leave. Perhaps he'd grown just as weary as I over the spats. Since he left, I seemed to have even less patience for the boys. You'd think that with Paul out of the house, all the friction would've gone with him. Then why did I sometimes catch myself snapping at the boys for silly things?

The ringing of the telephone interrupted my thoughts. A few minutes later, I heard Matthew calling, "Mom! Dad is on the phone and he wants to talk to you."

The thought of speaking to Paul made my heart flutter. Why did I feel a catch in my throat whenever he called? It seemed to happen more and more lately, even when I thought about him. And that quickened step to answer the phone, how do I explain that? Did I truly miss him or had loneliness begun to affect me? Perhaps he was merely a habit I was finding hard to break. If he were back in my life again, would I strive to do things differently? But doesn't it take two to make any relationship work? He'd have to want to change, as well. As I reached for the phone I realized how crazy my thoughts were. It was foolish to even think about this. After all, wasn't he the one who took a new job and moved out? He was probably much happier now that he was on his own.

"Hello, Paul." I hoped he couldn't detect the quickening in my voice.

"Hello, Julie. The boys asked me to talk to you."

"About what?"

"They'd like to go camping for their birthday again."

"They would?"

"I realize that it might be uncomfortable for us with our situation being the way it is, but perhaps we can put our own feelings aside and do this for the kids?"

"But will it be warm enough? It's only May."

"Our last camping trip was around the same time and it was fine. There's no reason to think that it won't be as warm this time."

I had to admit that despite everything that had happened between us, Paul tried to remain close to the boys. No one could fault him for not being a good father. A vision of our last camping trip floated back to my mind. I remember trying to argue against it. My idea of going camping had been to check into a room at a motel. The thought of sleeping on the ground in a tent didn't thrill me much, to say the least. But Paul talked me into it. "Don't disappoint the boys," he'd said. "They really want their mother to join in the fun."

"Fun? You call sleeping on the hard ground and offering oneself as fresh meat to all the insects around fun?"

He laughed. "It won't be that bad. Try it. If you don't like it, we won't do it again. I promise."

The camping trip had turned out to be an oasis of fun in what had been a continuous sea of arguments. Being separated and soon to be divorced, things would be uncomfortable for certain.

"I'm not sure this would work out." Being so close to you, I wanted to say, remembering how that romantic evening under the stars ended.

"We shouldn't disappoint the boys because of our

81

irreconcilable differences. It wouldn't be fair."

His choice of words echoed in my ears. It was obvious he thought there was no way for us to get back together. I wanted to say no and keep our distance, but knew I'd be letting the boys down. I realized that the separation itself, with their dad so far away, was difficult enough for them. To disappoint them by not going would only make matters worse.

Without warning, I heard myself reply, "You're right. The boys shouldn't suffer because of us. Let's go camping." I'd probably regret going, but it was only one weekend out of my life.

"Great! The boys will be so happy."

Paul sounded happy himself, but after what he said before, I was probably just reading something into his reaction.

We were all packed and ready to go when Paul honked. He came into the house to help us carry our stuff. He looked excited and happy, the way he used to look when we were going away together as a family. Our hands brushed as I handed him a bag. A jolt of excitement rushed through me and he seemed to react in the same manner. Had I not heard him tell me we had irreconcilable differences, I would've thought it possible that some old feelings were still alive.

When we arrived at the campsite, we began setting up. I admired Paul's ability to put things together. He didn't even need directions, whereas I was directionally challenged and could read them twenty times over and still not be able to follow them.

As soon as the tent was up, the twins began to clamor about going hiking.

"Come along with us, Julie. It will be fun," Paul said.

"I think I should get dinner prepared," I answered. The thought of encountering snakes and dangerous animals didn't have the same thrill for me.

While Paul and the boys were gone, I found myself thinking again. Being together as a family on this camping trip and seeing Matthew and Michael enjoying their father's company, I kept forgetting that we weren't together anymore.

I was quite glad that when the boys returned with Paul they didn't have any snakes with them. We barbecued franks and hamburgers; afterward the boys had birthday cake.

When it was time for bed, I put my sleeping bag on the other side of the boys. I'd given this a great deal of thought. Even though we were in separate sleeping bags, I just didn't feel comfortable putting it next to Paul's. I had no idea whether or not he felt the same. He didn't comment about it and put his sleeping bag down by the edge of the tent.

Despite all my original fears about going on this camping trip, it had been an enjoyable day. I closed my eyes and waited for sleep. I found myself listening to the quiet breathing of the twins, but hours passed and I was still wide-awake.

Quietly, I slipped out of my sleeping bag and went outside. It was a magnificent starry night. Realizing that I should've taken a blanket or sweater to ward off the slight chill, I wrapped my arms around myself.

"Couldn't sleep, either?" I heard Paul whisper behind me.

I turned to see him wrapped in a blanket. He sat down on an overturned log we were using as a chair.

"Join me before you catch cold."

I sat down right next to him and Paul wrapped the blanket around the both of us.

"I've really enjoyed myself being with you and the kids," he said.

"Me, too," I admitted.

"As I lay in the darkness, I suddenly remembered the night you went into labor."

"Oh, dear, why that day of all times to think about? That was such a horror show," I said, recalling the biggest comedy of errors I'd ever experienced in my life—except it wasn't too funny then.

"I don't know. It just made our relationship unique. I doubt if another couple had a similar experience."

I found it strange that he should bring it up now of all times.

"First I got stuck in traffic on my way home to get you."

"Then when you finally got there you discovered that the elevator was out of order."

"It was the first time I ever regretted living on the sixth floor," Paul said.

"I'll never forget the look of surprise on your face as we began our descent and my overnight case opened and everything spilled out down the steps," I said.

"That wasn't too funny."

"Nor was that walk down."

"I honestly didn't think you were going to make it."

"I know. My contractions were coming fast and furious and I'd get down half a flight before I had to sit another one out."

"I was so afraid you were going to give birth right there on the steps."

"At the rate I was going, it was quite possible, but I made it to the car."

"Only to find that we had a flat tire."

"I really felt sorry for you when you had to run back up the six flights to call a cab," I said.

"Yeah. That was a real bummer. But the biggest kicker was when we finally reached the hospital and the doctor examined you."

"By the look on your face, you were just as shocked as I was when he discovered the second heartbeat."

"I could never understand how the boys were able to fool the doctor by lying on top of one another."

"They were beautiful, though, and certainly worth every bit of trouble."

"That's for sure. Being together as a family made me realize what I'd been missing," he said as he reached for my hand under the blanket. "I really thought the new position was what I wanted with its higher salary and perks. I was wrong. The past few months have been so empty for me."

I turned to face him. My heart was nearly singing in accompaniment to his words.

"They haven't been the best for me, either. If it hadn't been for the boys, it would've been worse."

Paul gently squeezed my hand underneath the blanket. The pressure of his fingers on mine sent shivers of delight right through me. I hadn't felt that wonderful in such a long time. And I wanted that feeling to last beyond the moment.

"I've had a great deal of time to think and must've gone over everything at least a thousand times. If I had done this or if I had done that . . ."

"It wasn't just you, Paul. I was as much to blame."

"If I hadn't put work before you and the kids . . ."

"Perhaps I should've been more understanding and cooperative."

"I guess we both could've been more understanding and bothered to take the time to listen to one another."

"Yes, there had been hardly any communication between us. How could we allow things to snowball as they did?"

Paul dropped my hand and gently caressed my face as he looked into my eyes. I peered back into those beautiful eyes, the same ones I'd often find myself drowning in, as I did now. I heard him whisper, "I don't want to throw our love away."

"It's much too precious to let go."

"Does that mean that you want to try and put all this behind us?" Paul asked, drawing me close.

I smiled and a moment later he covered my mouth with his and tenderly kissed me. I kissed him back hungrily, wanting more and needing it. I couldn't remember the last time I was held in those strong arms of his as we rekindled our love under a sky of twinkling stars.

Driving home the next day as the boys happily chattered away, I wondered how Paul and I would work things out. I knew it was going to take a great deal of compromise, especially when it concerned where we'd live. At that moment, it occurred to me that I really didn't care if the kids and I remained in the house we were living in. What had seemed so important was no longer an issue. I was beginning to believe in my heart that no problem was insurmountable when love was involved. We'd come to the brink and were aware of what was at stake. We would be more careful.

Michael interrupted my thoughts by asking, "Dad, are we home yet?"

I turned to Paul. He was smiling. "Son, it doesn't matter where we are. Whenever all four of us are together, we're home."

THE END

LONG LOST LOVE
Why did he come back now?

"**I** shouldn't have given you the message," my sister said. "You're getting married in three weeks. The last thing you should be thinking about is Marty Davidson."

We were in the fitting room of a local bridal store, waiting for the seamstress. Rita was wearing a long dark blue velvet dress, the dress she was to wear as matron of honor at my wedding. She looked at my expression and put her hands on her hips. "Tell me you aren't thinking of returning his call!"

I was thinking of doing just that. Marty was my first husband. I hadn't seen him in thirteen years. I realized now that, deep down, I'd been waiting for this call all that time. I'd moved to a nearby town five years ago, but Rita was still in the book, so Marty had called her.

"He walked out on me without a word," I said. "He left me nothing but a note and debts and a positive pregnancy test. I have a few things to say to him."

"Please, Claudia," she begged. "You never could resist that guy."

"I can resist him," I said. The minute I said the words I wondered if they were true.

"What's Tom going to say?"

"I don't know, but I feel like I have to do this. Did Marty say how long he'd be here?"

"No. Knowing him, it won't be long."

An hour later, I called Marty from the coffee shop where Rita and I had lunch. My heart gave a little lurch when his familiar voice answered the phone.

"You sound wonderful," he said.

"What are you doing here?" I asked, my tone abrupt.

"I'm staying with my brother," he said. I remembered Marty's brother. It had taken me five years to get an address out of him so I could send Marty divorce papers. I didn't even try to get child support.

Marty cleared his throat. "I wondered if you'd have dinner with me."

I didn't answer.

"For old time's sake," he said. His voice dropped. "I've thought about you often. And I want to talk to you about Jodie." Jodie was our daughter. Marty had left before he even knew she was on the way. Jodie had never gotten so much as a birthday card from Marty.

"Okay," I said harshly. "I want to talk to you, too."

As I walked the six blocks across town to Tom's office, I began regretting my decision. It had taken me a long time to get over Marty's sudden desertion. A year ago, I'd met Tom, a widower nearing forty who owned a construction business. He was sweet, trustworthy, and loyal. Everything that Marty hadn't been.

Tom and I were planning an evening candlelight wedding. We told ourselves it was for Jodie, who was delighted at the idea of a large formal wedding. The truth was that Tom and I were having fun planning every detail.

Marty and I had eloped. Marty didn't like to plan anything and besides, he pointed out, my parents didn't like him. We'd been married in some ugly town hall in the next state by a clerk who didn't look much older than us.

"It doesn't matter, honey," Marty said. "On our twentieth wedding anniversary, we'll have the whole county over for a barbeque when we renew our vows." Seven months later he was gone.

Why was I having dinner with him? Did I want to see Marty to clear the air, or was that just an excuse to see him? I began to hope Tom would insist I call Marty and cancel dinner.

"The wedding dinner menu came," Tom said, standing up behind his desk and holding one up. His eyes twinkled. He was no match in looks for Marty, but I was happy to see his familiar, kind face.

"Great," I said, taking the typed menu and looking it over carefully. When I looked up, Tom was staring at me.

"What's up?" he asked. Tom could read me perfectly.

I sank into a chair and he sat down. "Marty is in town. I told him I'd have dinner with him."

He nodded. I remembered how angry he'd become when I told him how Marty had hurt me.

"I won't go if you don't want me to," I said, hoping he'd insist that I cancel.

Tom looked at me quietly for a minute. "I want you for my wife very much, Linda. But I want you to be absolutely sure that's what you want, too."

I swallowed. "Okay."

"I'll be home doing some paperwork, if you need me. Are you taking Jodie?"

"No! I'm not even going to tell her where I'm going. I don't know what I'll do if he wants to see her. He probably has legal rights."

Tom looked worried. He wanted to adopt Jodie during the coming summer, so she could go into the eighth grade at a new school with her new name. Jodie was very excited about having a father.

I didn't fuss with my looks for the dinner. That seemed too disloyal to Tom. As I went through my closet, I saw the mauve velvet Victorian-style gown I had picked for my wedding gown. I found an appropriate dress for the restaurant Marty had picked, the best restaurant in town. Jodie came into the room as I was changing.

"Gee, Mom, that's an old dress."

"It's still good. Don't forget to take your homework to Gran's."

"There's going to be an ice storm. Do you have to go?"

I'd told Jodie that I was having dinner with someone I'd known in high school. That was true enough. "I'll be careful, honey," I said.

When we got to my mother's, she had to add her two cents. Drawing me aside, she said, "You know your father never liked Marty." Dad had died last year.

"Neither did you."

"He wasn't a solid kind of man."

I felt an absurd impulse to defend Marty, as I had years ago. "He wasn't even a man. He was twenty. Most people aren't solid citizens yet at twenty."

"You know exactly what I mean, Linda. He was wild."

I sighed. Even all these years later, I couldn't explain to my mother that Marty's wildness was part of his attraction when I was twenty.

It was too warm now for snow, but the rain coming down as I drove to the restaurant was more ice than water. I drove carefully, and I got there a little late.

Marty was waiting for me, rising from his chair, as the maitre d' led me toward him. I caught my breath. Marty's dazzling smile was the same. He was tall and broad-shouldered and wearing an expensive suit. Thirteen years had only improved his looks. The smile lines around his eyes just made him better looking. His eyes were exactly the color of Jodie's.

"You grew up to be a lovely woman," he said, still standing.

That took some more of the wind out of my sails, and I couldn't think of anything to say. The waiter came and held my chair. We sat down.

"Let's have some dinner before we talk," he said.

"I'm not very hungry."

"I'll order something light," he said, motioning to the waiter. Thirteen years had taught him about wine and how to order from a French menu. That didn't seem to go with the Marty who used to drive a motorcycle and listen to country music.

Somehow we got through dinner. I felt self-conscious, like I was out on a first date. I kept looking for all that anger I'd stored up, since it made a good shield, but mostly I was stunned by the grown-up Marty. He talked about his travels for much of dinner. He asked questions about my job. He asked gently about Jodie. I bragged about her. Finally, coffee came.

"To start with, let's agree I was a rat," he said with a charming grin.

I remembered all the times Marty had quit jobs or stayed out with his friends, and then charmed me out of being mad at him. I felt my anger flare. "Rat sounds too nice. Let's agree that you were cruel, irresponsible, and abandoned your wife and baby."

"Linda, be fair. I didn't know about any baby when I left." He calmly took a sip of his coffee. "As for the rest, I was twenty years old and stupid."

He was echoing my own words to my mother. "You were twenty when you left," I retorted. "You were twenty-five when Jodie was five, and I know you knew about her by then. You were thirty when she was ten. So that excuse doesn't hold water, does it? I can forgive you for acting the way you did toward me. I'll never forgive you for ignoring our daughter."

His eyes turned sad. "No, I wouldn't blame you." He sighed and looked off into the distance. "I thought about her and I thought about you. Often. I felt like I didn't know how to explain, and I still don't. I felt like I had to somehow be able to make it up to you both, like come back with lots of money to help you. Then when I finally got money, I realized that was just an excuse for being too scared to face you."

"You know, Marty, that's a touching confession, but Jodie has gone most of her childhood without a father. Now I'm about to marry someone else. He wants to adopt her. Then you just show up like a bad penny."

His eyes widened. "You're getting married?"

"Did you think we'd just be waiting here for you, nothing changed? Like some fairy-tale princess, waiting for the prince?"

"Maybe I did think something like that," he said slowly. "I had so many daydreams about this over the years. I did something dumb when I was young, and apparently it changed my life forever."

I didn't know what to say to that. I was surprised to find that

I actually felt sorry for him. "It's getting late," I said.

"I'd like to meet Jodie and spend some time with her."

"I don't know, Marty."

"If you give me your number, I'll call you in the morning. You can think about it overnight."

I gave him my number and we gathered our things and left. The sleet had stopped, but the parking lot was a sheet of ice. Marty took my arm, and a tremor went through me.

"Let me drive you home," he said.

I pulled my arm away. The feeling of attraction I had toward him made me abrupt. "I'll be okay." I charged ahead, almost falling.

"I'll follow you home," he said to my back.

The streets were very slippery, and I couldn't stop looking back in my rear-view mirror at the lights behind me. Before I even realized what had happened, I'd skidded across the road and into a ditch. I was going so slowly that when I came to a stop in the ditch with my foot on the brake, my airbag didn't even inflate. I stared out the window at the cockeyed headlights, my heart pounding.

"Linda!" The passenger side door opened.

"I'm okay," I said. "I had my seatbelt on."

"I've got you." He clicked open the seatbelt and drew me across the passenger seat, into his arms. When he got me outside, he picked me up.

"Marty, I'm fine." My heart was still beating wildly, but I wasn't sure of the cause anymore. He carried me across the road and put me gently into the passenger side of his rental car.

"Fasten your seatbelt," he said, smoothing my hair back. "I'm going to turn out your lights and lock up your car."

He was back in a minute and got in his side. He turned to me in the darkness, putting his arm around my shoulder. "I was terrified when I saw you lose control. To have found you and then to lose you again!" His voice was hoarse. I could smell his aftershave and I felt lightheaded. I didn't think it was from the accident.

"Could you take me home, please," I said in a small voice. "It's left at the next corner."

At my house, Marty helped me up the walkway. "I'm fine," I said. He stopped at the steps. "Linda . . ."

The bushes were covered with ice and they glittered in the porch light. I had an odd, out-of-time feeling, like I was in a fairy tale, like I was the seventeen-year-old in love with handsome Marty Davidson and yet myself now, too. He took me in his arms and kissed me. A thrill went through my body.

"No!" I pulled away. I ran up the steps, only to slip and fall into his arms again. I felt excited, attracted, and panicked all at the same time.

"It's okay," he said softly, righting me. "I'll call you tomorrow morning."

Inside the house, I sat for fifteen minutes, waiting for my heart to slow. Then I called for a tow truck. Then I called my mother to ask her to keep Jodie overnight.

"Is he there?" my mother asked.

"Of course not."

"You don't have to act insulted. He was the kind of boy who got his way with girls."

"I'm not a girl anymore."

"You sound funny."

"I had a little accident on the ice. I'm okay. I think even the car is okay, but it's stuck in a ditch."

I put down the phone, and I knew I'd have to call Tom. He sounded relieved to hear my voice.

"He wants to see Jodie. I haven't told her yet."

"You'll have to tell her. And she has to meet him. This isn't something you can keep from her. The sooner the better."

"I guess."

"What kind of reaction did you have to him?"

I was silent.

He sighed. "I was hoping you'd say you didn't know what you ever saw in him." He gave a little laugh.

"Tom, I . . ."

"What?"

"I was still attracted to him."

"You know, we drove all the way into the city to see that play with that actor you're crazy about."

Why was he talking about this? "Yes. So?"

"You're attracted to that actor, aren't you?"

"What's your point?"

"My point is, don't take it too seriously, honey. I love you." He hung up.

In the morning, the ice had all melted and the sun was shining. It wasn't spring yet, but it wouldn't be long. My mechanic had left my car in my driveway. It had a dent in the fender that went well with the rust. I'd been saving for a new used car all year.

I went and picked up Jodie, but I couldn't think of how to bring up the subject of Marty. I was down in the basement doing laundry when I heard the phone ring. Jodie didn't call me, so I figured it was one of her friends.

When I came up from the basement, Jodie had the kitchen

91

phone in her hand. Her eyes were round and she looked very happy. "He says he's Marty Davidson. He says he's my dad." She held out the phone.

I felt angry with Marty for a minute, and then I shrugged. That was Marty. I arranged for us to meet him for lunch.

I was irritated with myself when I realized that I was preparing for our date with Marty with much more care than the night before. Jodie kept running in and out of my room with different outfits, dithering about what to wear. I was dithering myself.

By the time we got to the restaurant, Jodie was quieter and more self-conscious. By the time we got to the table, I could see she was feeling very shy.

Marty quickly ended that. "You're all grown up," he said, to her delight. "You're a lovely young woman."

Marty charmed her all the way through the meal. He told her adventure stories about where he'd traveled. He told stories that made him look silly and funny. By the time we were done eating, they were exchanging jokes and giggling.

"Let's all do something this afternoon," Marty said to me.

"I can't. I'm supposed to meet Tom at the new house." Tom had put a down payment on a house for us. It would be the first house in my life that I hadn't rented. We were supposed to pick paint colors today. I wanted to see him. I wanted to see what I felt. At the moment, I was feeling very confused.

"Can Jodie come with me?" Marty asked. "I'll bring her home later."

I looked at Jodie, who looked excited. Marty winked at her.

"Home by three?" I asked. "A couple of hours only. Jodie has homework."

"I promise," Marty said.

Outside the house that Tom and I were to share, I sat gathering my courage. Tom's car was in the driveway, so he was inside. It was a cute house, not too big but with a porch and a picket fence. I'd always wanted a picket fence. It meant security and home to me, and a husband I could count on. Now I felt like I might be throwing all that away.

Tom was sitting on the stairs in the front hall, waiting for me. He was wearing jeans and a blue shirt with the sleeves rolled up. His jacket hung on the banister post. I looked at his strong forearms and his big shoulders and his kind eyes, and I went to him. He folded me in his arms.

"You know," he said, holding me to him, still sitting on the stairs, "I've been hoping that you'd remember that whatever else I am to you, I'm your friend."

"My best friend," I said, talking into his neck.

"Yes. I won't say some phony baloney like all I want is your happiness. I want my happiness, too. But I do want you to be sure what you want."

"I don't understand why I find him so attractive, especially after what he did."

"I've seen his picture. He's a good-looking guy. He's the first guy you loved and the first guy you had sex with. He's the father of your daughter. And he hasn't been around all these years for you to take him for granted or even be irritated with him. He's romantic."

"Why are you so understanding? If it was the other way around, I'd be throwing a fit."

"I'll throw a fit if it will help."

"I love you," I said.

"I know. I love you, too. I hope that's enough."

We sat there for a long time in the afternoon.

"I don't think this is a good day to pick paint," Tom said finally. "I'll walk you to your car." He kissed my hand.

Jodie was home when I got there. "Marty, I mean Daddy . . ." She looked confused. "He told me to call him Daddy. He wanted to take me out to dinner, but I told you'd be worried and I had to go home. He said he'd call you tonight."

"That's right, I'd have been worried. I'll make some hot chocolate."

When we sat down at the kitchen table, Jodie looked pensive.

"So, how do you like him?" I asked.

"Oh, I like him a lot," she said. She took a sip of her cocoa. "He said that he'd always loved you and maybe you guys would get married again."

"What!"

"Well, then he said I shouldn't mention that to you. He said he might want that but you might not realize yet that you were meant to be together. He said it was like a daydream, and did I have daydreams." She looked away from me. "I said I had daydreams for a lot of years when I was little that he'd suddenly come back and that he'd be handsome and fun and want to be with me. Just like what happened."

I felt a lump in my throat. "What did he say then?"

"He said he was sorry he hadn't come sooner, that he had to make his fortune first. I thought people only said that in stories, 'make your fortune.' Then he said that I was a daughter to be proud of." She giggled. "That used to be part of my daydream, too!"

93

I laughed with her, but I felt like I could cry, too.

"I like him," she said, with a troubled expression, "but I like Tom better. Is that bad?"

"However you feel is the right way to feel, sweetie. Why do you like Tom better?"

"It's hard to explain. Marty, I mean Daddy . . . he's like a movie star. But then when you get home, it's like getting home from the movies. It's not real, not like real life."

I stared at her, astonished. How had I raised such a wise child with so little wisdom myself?

"Tom, he's not like a daydream or the movies," she explained, getting up to put her cup in the sink. "I know I can count on him. And I know he loves me because he knows what I'm really like. He's proud of me because of things I actually do—like I play basketball well and I get good grades in math. I'm not a daydream to him; I'm a real person. I can't explain it."

I got up and hugged her. "You explained very well." I went and got my coat. "How about you start defrosting that chicken? I have an errand to run."

It didn't surprise me that Marty had the biggest, fanciest room at the old renovated Victorian hotel. I called up from the desk and he had a big smile and two drinks waiting.

"How did you get away?" he asked, as though being with my daughter was some kind of duty for me.

"I'm just staying a minute, Marty. I wanted to correct something you said to Jodie today about the possibility of us getting together again. That isn't going to happen. I love Tom. I'm going to marry him in three weeks."

He put down his drink and walked up to stand close in front of me. I looked up into his gorgeous eyes. He ran his hand down my face and then down my arm.

"And what about that?" he whispered.

"That is only chemistry, Marty." I pushed him away. "A woman can have chemistry with a number of men. That's nature. It counts, but it isn't all that counts. Love counts. Trust counts. Loyalty counts."

"I've lost you."

"You lost me long ago. I'm just a daydream you have sometimes when you're lonely. You don't know me anymore. You know the girl I was at twenty. And it's only memory that's been happening to us last night and today." I smiled. "Plus a little chemistry."

"I don't guess there's much to hold me here if you don't want me," he said.

94

I felt a surge of anger, but I reminded myself I was dealing with Marty. "There's your daughter."

He looked at me sadly. "She talked about Tom constantly. Tom this, Tom that."

"That's good, Marty," I said gently, "because he's going to be her father. She needs somebody to count on while she finishes growing up, and I don't think that's you. That doesn't mean you can't be part of her life."

He nodded, but his gaze was already drifting out the window, looking toward faraway places. I turned and left.

Night had fallen when I got back to the house. Tom and Jodie were playing checkers in the living room.

"Uh, I've got homework. Call me when dinner is ready," Jodie said, and ran up the stairs.

"Are you hungry?" I asked him.

"Yes." He smiled. "That sounds so domestic. I came over to act like a caveman."

"How does a caveman act?"

He went into a monkey stance for a moment, and we both laughed. "I guess I'm out of practice. I'm supposed to tell you you're my woman, and club you over the head until you agree, then drag you back to the cave by your hair." He looked at me, eyes unsure. "I didn't feel like I was putting up enough of a battle for you."

"You don't have to battle. I think Marty will be gone by tomorrow. If not, we'll invite him to the wedding."

"Oh, shoot," Tom said, pulling me into his arms. "I was all ready to do battle. Guess I'll have to make love not war." He kissed me.

"Plenty of chemistry there, too," I murmured.

"What?"

"Never mind. Kiss me again."

THE END

95

"I WANT TO BE A DECENT MAN!"
A Beautiful Story About The Hope Of Redemption.

It was May, the season of new beginnings. All along Wheeler Street, the trees were starting to leaf out, and dandelions had blossomed in the cracks between the sidewalks. I stood in front of house number 366—Tammy's house, clinging to the slim hope that it wasn't too late, that we could somehow make a new beginning, too.

I walked up onto the porch with my heart in my throat and my hat in my hands. Up until then, I'd thought of myself as a big man, at six-feet-two and a couple hundred pounds. But at that moment, I felt about six inches tall. I'd just been released from prison, and I knew that Tammy was not going to be pleased to see me, but I'd come three years and a hundred and thirty-five miles to get to this moment. Now, there was no turning back, so I swallowed a deep breath and knocked on the door.

I heard footsteps inside, and mentally went over the speech I'd spent three years preparing. The door opened; I caught a flash of Tammy's strawberry-blond hair, and the blur of her white T-shirt before the door started to slam shut again. Before it closed completely, I jammed my foot inside.

"Tammy, wait!"

"You get out of here!"

"I just want to talk to you for a minute!"

"I mean it, Luke! Get out, or I'm calling the cops!"

I pushed the door open and shoved myself inside. Tammy was already headed for the phone. "Why can't we just talk for a minute?"

"Because I have nothing to say to you! And you've got nothing to say that I want to hear!" She grabbed up the phone and started punching in numbers. I could see it in her eyes, then—how much she hated me.

I can't say I blamed her, after all the things I'd done.

I used to think about it a lot, lying in my prison cell at night: How hard Tammy tried. Little details would come back to me—things I hadn't appreciated at the time, like bouquets of wildflowers on the kitchen table, and blackberry pies cooling on the windowsill, their purple juice staining Tammy's hands. Crisp, white sheets hanging on the clothesline, smelling like fresh air and sunshine, and the same sweet scent in Tammy's hair. Lying in my cell, these memories haunted me. They caused a terrible aching in my chest, a yearning to go back, to somehow undo all the terrible things I'd done to Tammy, just because I could. Hating women came naturally to me, but, then—

I'd had a lot of practice.

The first one I encountered, naturally, was my mother, though I barely remember her. She dumped me off at my grandmother's house when I was four and never came back for me. Well, that's okay, a person might think—a little boy being raised by his grandmother, that's just fine. Except that my grandma was no sweet little old lady. She was a tough-talking, hard-drinking old broad who often left me alone while she went out to drink at the American Legion, or to play Bingo down at the fire hall. When I was thirteen, Grandma died of cirrhosis of the liver, and then Social Services came and packed me off to a state-run farm for boys.

The farm was no picnic in the park, believe me. There were two-dozen boys living there, ranging in age from nine to eighteen years old. We had to fight each other for every inch of turf we gained, so it wasn't exactly one big happy family. We got enough food to keep us alive, lumpy beds to sleep in, and not much else, except for a lot of hard work. We attended Martin Van Buren School, where we were treated like outcasts. I'd hear other kids making plans to go bowling after school, or out to Pizza Hut, and I'd sit there in my Salvation Army clothes, hating my mother and wishing I had a real family, a normal life.

At sixteen, I fell in love with a cheerleader named Angela Garrett. Angela had long, brown hair and big, sensuous lips, and a figure that made it real hard for me to concentrate on English literature, which was the only class I was in with her. I would sit at the desk behind hers, getting high on her perfume and dreaming up ways to ask her out. I didn't consider myself a bad-looking dude; I was taller than most, and ripped from working on the farm. Oh, I knew I didn't stand a chance with Angela, but something in the way she smiled at me, and giggled with her friends whenever I walked by, made me fool enough to try.

Our house parents, Bob and Eileen Mackie, used to give us three dollars a week for pocket money. I saved my money from September to Christmas, which is how long it took me to finally get up my nerve. Then, on the day before Christmas break, when Angela was standing at her locker, alone, I gathered up my nerve and approached her.

97

"Hey, Angela," I said, stuffing my trembling hands into my pockets.

"Hey," she replied, barely looking at me.

I shot a glance up and down the hallway. There were more people hanging around than I would've liked; I mean, it was going to be a heck of a long walk back to my locker if Angela said no. But knowing it was now or never, I cleared my throat and finally spit it out.

"Um, would you go to the movies with me sometime, over break?"

By this point, Angela was staring at me, and she definitely wasn't smiling. "Are you asking me out?" she asked, loud enough for everyone to hear.

I felt the heat prickling up the back of my neck. I knew right then that it'd been a mistake to even ask. Please, I begged silently, don't humiliate me.

"Yeah, I, umm, I g-guess I am."

"Get a clue, Luke!" she shouted. "Cheerleaders do not go out with guys who wear high-water pants!" As if she hadn't already shamed me enough, she added, "And girls who live on Plymouth Avenue don't go to the movies with wards of the state!"

I didn't ask another girl out for two more years.

Then at eighteen, with no money and nowhere else to go, I joined the Army. I stayed in for four years; I was twenty-two when I met Tammy. She was eighteen at the time, and working at her family's gas station near the base, where I often went to buy beer and lottery tickets. Tammy isn't beautiful; her best feature is her long, strawberry-blond hair, which she wore back then tied back with a pink ribbon. No, ma'am, I'd gone to bed with some real hotties during my Army career, and Tammy wasn't one of them. But she was soft looking, and innocent, and she kept her mouth shut and did as she was told, so I decided to take her out and have some fun with her for a while.

As it turned out, Tammy came from even less than I did. Her family lived in a dilapidated apartment above their gas station. Tammy pumped gas, sold lottery tickets, and kept house for her two older brothers and her drunken parents. She had zero hope for anything better in life until I came along. I thought I was a big man, of course. I drank hard, I talked mean, and I fought dirty. For some reason that I have honestly never been able to fathom, Tammy loved me.

I didn't like the discipline of Army life, so when my four years were up, I decided not to reenlist. Shortly before my discharge, one of my ex-Army buddies, Rod, emailed me from Ohio. He was working for his uncle, installing vinyl siding. He said his uncle was looking to hire a couple of guys. I didn't have a better plan for my life, so I decided to check it out. I decided to take Tammy with me, too, because I figured life was easier with her than without her. A week later, I bought a secondhand car, threw my discharge papers and my clothes into my duffel bag, and drove over to Tammy's place.

"Pack your things, baby," I told her. "We're getting out of here."

She stared at me, wide-eyed. "To where?"

"Rod came through with the job in Ohio. I start next week."

"I can't go with you, Luke," she said softly. "Not unless you marry me."

I stared at her like she was crazy. "Come on, baby. You know I love you. We don't need a piece of paper to prove it, do we?"

Tammy had never stood up to me before, but that time, she stood her ground, saying that if she left with me and it didn't work out, her father would never let her come back.

Like I said before, I didn't really love Tammy, but at least she made my life comfortable.

What the heck? I thought. How bad could it be?

Three days later, Tammy and I stood in front of a judge and got the piece of paper she was so worried about. Then we packed everything we owned into my car and headed for Ohio.

It took us four days to get there. I remember lying in a sleeping bag under the stars at night, Tammy's head resting on my chest.

"What's it going to be like in Ohio, Luke?" she asked me, at least a hundred times. And every time she asked, I filled her head with fairy tales, and made promises I never intended to keep.

When we got to Ohio, we rented a singlewide trailer on a dirt road five miles outside of town. We only had one car, so Tammy couldn't go anywhere without me, and that suited me just fine.

I hated my new job, and I got bored with married life real fast. I'd come home from work at night, eat my dinner, play around in bed with Tammy for a while, and then go out and hit the bars with Rod. Tammy never said a word, but I knew that my behavior hurt her. She tried hard to make a decent home for us, but it seemed like the harder she tried, the more miserable I became. It got worse and worse, until one day, when I actually physically abused her.

It was hot that day. I came home from work feeling tired and irritable. The air conditioner wasn't working and the trailer felt like an incinerator, but as usual, Tammy greeted me at the door with a kiss and a smile. I grabbed a beer from the refrigerator and sat down at the table. Tammy pulled our dinner out of the oven and set it before me.

"What's this?" I asked.

"Macaroni and cheese."

"We just had macaroni and cheese last week."

"I know, Luke—I'm sorry. I had to scrimp a little this week."

"What did you do with the money I gave you for groceries?"

"Your check was short last week, remember?"

I remembered all too well, actually, because it'd been one of the worst hangovers I'd ever had. I'd told Tammy that I'd lost a day due to a work shortage, but actually, I'd called in sick and spent the day in a bar. Now, Tammy was looking at me like she suspected as much, but I knew she would never dare accuse me.

She made me angry, just the same.

"I can't help it if there's no work, Tammy. I don't control the weather," I said nastily. "But when a man does put in a hard day's work, he doesn't expect to come home and sit down to crappy macaroni and cheese!"

"I'm sorry, Luke," Tammy repeated softly, with her head down and big, fat tears rolling down her cheeks.

For some reason, those tears threw me into a rage. "Look at this junk! It's completely burned!" I swept my arm across the tabletop, knocking the casserole onto the floor.

"Do you want me to make you a sandwich?" Tammy squeaked, trying hard not to cringe, but I could see she was doing it instinctively.

"A sandwich? Oh, that would be just perfect, Tammy!" I spat sarcastically. Then I stood up and headed for the door. "You're worthless, Tammy. Do you know that?"

"Wh-where are you going?"

"Out."

Meekly, she followed after me, still crying. "Please, Luke—d-don't go. Sit down and drink your beer. I'll make you something else for dinner—something better—something you'll like."

"Don't bother. And don't wait up for me, either!"

But Tammy was desperate; somehow, even though I could tell she was afraid of me, she kept right on coming. Maybe she was more afraid of never seeing me again, because she clung to me, begging me not to leave her alone. I shoved her away, causing her to fall to the floor. Then, when she got back up and tried to reach for me again, I hit her in the face with my open hand. Up until then, I'd only abused her with my words, but after that night, hurting her physically became second nature to me.

When we'd been in Ohio for about a year, Tammy told me

that she was pregnant. I screamed at her like she'd done something wrong; I even accused her of messing around with other men. That was the last time I ever saw her cry; it was like I'd finally wrung the last tear out of her.

I wasn't happy about having a kid on the way, and I sure didn't make Tammy's pregnancy any easier for her. I was impatient with her mood swings, and I cut her no slack at all when it came to her wifely duties. Then after her fourth month, her doctor said that sex was unadvisable for the duration of her pregnancy, so I started messing around with other women. The night Tammy gave birth to Tyler, I was in a motel room with some bimbo I'd met in a bar.

I didn't lift a finger to help Tammy raise Tyler. I was jealous of the time she spent with him, of the love she used to give me so freely that she now lavished on our son. Naturally, I started spending even more time away from home.

Then when Tyler was two years old, I got into a barroom brawl. I hit a guy in the head with a broken beer bottle and spent the next three years in jail for assault. That's when I started to rethink my life. I guess you could say that I finally found out what it feels like to be belittled, to have someone twice your size beat up on you, just because they can. In the meantime, somehow, Tammy scraped together the money to divorce me while I was incarcerated.

Prison changes a man. Some men get meaner and some find God, but no man ever comes away unchanged. Three years certainly gave me a lot of time to think about my life, that's for sure. I was twenty-nine years old and Tammy and Tyler were the only family I had. And now, when it was too late, I realized that they were also the only family I wanted. On the outside, I'd barely given my kid a second thought, but suddenly, locked up behind bars, I was obsessed with him, wondering what he looked like, and whether he was rough-and-tumble, like his old man, or a bookworm, like Tammy.

When I got released from prison, I tracked Tammy down through the Internet. She'd moved out of the trailer, by then; she was living in a small house on Wheeler Street, and working as a teaching assistant at Tyler's elementary school. I called her on the phone a bunch of times, but she kept hanging up on me, so finally, I screwed up my nerve and went to see her.

Standing in her living room, that May afternoon, I saw that Tammy was not the same scared little girl I'd married and left behind. Time had turned Tammy into a beautiful woman—or maybe it was motherhood that had changed her. She'd gone from being rail-thin to being merely slender, with soft curves in all the right places. She'd had her hair cut into a short, chic style, and she was even wearing a little bit of makeup, which I'd never allowed her to do. But the change went deeper than that; I stared at her, trying to nail it down. Finally, it occurred to me:

Tammy's innocence was gone.

"Tammy, please put down the phone. I don't want to make trouble for you. I just want to see my son."

She turned on me, reeling, her eyes shooting daggers as she glared at me. "And just what gives you the right to come barging in here, making demands? Where do you get off, Luke?"

"I know I don't have any rights—not after the way I've treated you." My voice broke. "I just want to see my son—just once, Tammy. Then I'll leave."

She hesitated, giving me the courage to go on.

"I don't expect you to believe this, but I've changed, Tammy— I'll play by your rules from now on, whatever you say. I'm begging you, Tammy—just, please . . . let me see Tyler."

My breath rushed out of my chest in relief when she put the phone back in its cradle. It turned out that Tyler was playing at a friend's house that day, but Tammy was good enough to agree to let me see him the following weekend. Of course, she made it clear as water that she was only doing it for Tyler's sake, because he kept asking about me, and in fact, she told me in no uncertain terms that if I got out of line even as much as just once, I'd never see my son again.

Driving over there the following Sunday, I was thanking God that Tyler was too young to remember what a sad excuse I'd been for a father. I was also praying that God would help me not screw up again. I knew there was a lot riding on this visit; I pulled up in front of Tammy's house with my heart in my throat.

When Tyler appeared at the front door looking just like a miniature version of me, my heart swelled up with so much love for him, I thought I'd start crying and never be able to stop.

"Hey, buddy," I croaked.

He hid behind Tammy, not answering me. I fumbled with the Toys-R-Us bag I'd brought. "Come on out, buddy. I brought you something."

Hesitantly, he came outside, still clinging to his mother. Tammy nodded gently and gave him an encouraging smile, and that's when he finally shyly took the bag from my hand. He pulled out the little remote control racecar tucked inside and examined it.

"Do you like it?" I asked him.

He nodded, not looking at me.

"I thought we could run it here on the sidewalk." I squatted down to his level, forcing him to meet my gaze. "Dad wants to spend some time with you, Tyler. Did your mom tell you that?"

He nodded again, solemnly.

"It's almost lunchtime. How about if we go to McDonald's?"

His eyes filled with fear and he shook his head.

"You've got to be kidding me, buddy!" I tried to keep my tone light, despite the disappointment that was pooling in my chest. "I didn't think there was a little kid alive who'd turn down a cheeseburger and a chocolate milkshake!"

"I don't wanna go." He looked up at Tammy. "Do I have to go, Mama?"

"Of course you don't have to go." Tammy glanced at me, and then back at Tyler. "I've got an idea. How about if Dad drives over to McDonald's and brings the cheeseburgers back here? The two of you can have a little picnic right here on the porch."

After what seemed like an eternity, Tyler finally agreed to the plan. I slowly let out the breath I'd been holding and looked at Tammy with admiration. I was so happy I could've kissed her, but I knew she'd clobber me if I tried.

After that rough start, all in all, the visit went pretty smoothly. While we ate our cheeseburgers out on the porch, I tried to draw Tyler out. I wanted to know everything about him, but Tyler wasn't giving anything away. It wasn't until we started playing with the remote control car that he finally opened up to me a little, chattering away about school, and the great aquarium they had in his classroom, and his best friend, Jimmy Jankowitz. All too soon, though, Tammy came out and said it was time for Tyler to come inside.

"I'll come and see you again next week, okay, dude?" I said to Tyler, but my eyes were locked on Tammy's. Then she nodded a little, and I knew I was over the first hurdle.

I couldn't remember when a week had ever passed so slowly. My parole officer had set me up with a job unloading trucks at a food storage warehouse. It was boring and backbreaking work, but it helped pass the long hours between Sundays. I spent every minute thinking about Tyler and Tammy, looking forward to when I could be with them again. I spent half of my first paycheck on a small aquarium and some tropical fish for Tyler.

I started seeing him every weekend, but only during supervised visits at Tammy's house. I started building my relationship with my son, one small step at a time. I tried to get close to Tammy, too, even though she'd made it plain that she wanted nothing to do with me. I started fixing things for her around the house, and buying flowers for her little garden. But I knew it was going to take a lot more than that to win her back.

As it was, Tammy was going out with some geek named Neil, who was a math teacher at the school where she worked. I was jealous as hell, but I stayed cool. I even started babysitting Tyler on Saturday nights so Tammy and Neil could go out. One Saturday, I made plans to take Tyler to the movies. Tyler begged Tammy to go, too, and finally, she agreed. I spent the whole ninety minutes of that film sitting beside her, inhaling her sweet scent and aching to touch her. After the movie, we went back to her house and drank lemonade out on the porch. Everything was going just fine until she mentioned Neil. Then Tyler looked up from the Digimon cards he was playing with.

"Dad says Neil is a sissy."

Tammy's face reddened in anger. "Do you need your mouth washed out with soap, young man?"

Tyler stared down at his shoes. "No, Mama."

"We don't use words like that around here. Now, go to your room, Tyler."

After Tyler had slunk into the house, Tammy turned on me. "Nice work, Luke."

"I'm sorry."

"No, you're not." She got up and went inside, slamming the door shut behind her.

Two Saturdays later, Tyler was invited to an overnight birthday party. I stopped by the house, anyway, planning to give Tammy the excuse that I wanted to re-caulk the sink and tub in Tyler's bathroom.

When I got there, Tammy was sitting on the couch in her bathrobe with half a bottle of wine on the coffee table in front of her. Looking at her swollen face and red eyes, I had a pretty good idea about where the other half of the wine had gone. She didn't kick me out right off the bat, like I thought she would, so I went ahead with my spiel.

"I thought I'd get at that sink and tub tonight," I told her, "unless you have plans to go out or something."

"I don't have any plans to go out." She took a swallow of wine. "Neil broke up with me."

I had to work hard to keep the happiness from showing on my face. "Gee, Tammy—that's too bad."

"Yes, it is."

"Did he give you a reason?"

"Yes, Luke, he did. In fact, you're the reason. He can't handle the fact that I'm letting you see Tyler. He thinks you're a bad influence, and he's also afraid that you and I are going to get back together." She let out a short, sharp, mirthless bark of laughter. "As if I'd let you touch me with your ten-foot pole."

She'd misspoken, and her Freudian slip caused me to chuckle.

"Don't you laugh at me!" Her eyes brimmed with tears suddenly. "Don't you dare laugh at me, Luke Wilson!"

I couldn't bear her tears; they wiped the smile right off my face. "I'm sorry, Tammy. Do you want me to talk to Neil?"

"No. It was just an excuse, anyway. His real problem is that he doesn't want to make a commitment to me." She refilled her wineglass. "I don't know what it is about me that I attract such losers."

I knew it was a potshot at me, but one that I deserved, so I took it on the chin. Tammy held out the wine bottle to me.

"Care to drown your sorrows with me?"

"I don't drink anymore, Tammy."

"Well, I guess you really have turned over a new leaf, then, after all, haven't you?" she said, sarcasm dripping from her voice. "Jeez, Luke—you were such a bastard."

"I know I was."

"Nothing I ever did was good enough for you."

"It was me that wasn't good enough. I didn't love you then, Tammy—I admit that. But I love you now." I went and knelt before her and timidly reached over and caressed her cheek. "I love you now, Tammy," I whispered.

When she didn't pull away from me, I leaned in close and kissed her.

That kiss was like every dream I ever had coming true all at once. I'd never thought I'd taste the sweetness of Tammy's lips again, and suddenly, I was desperate to keep the moment from ending.

Finally, though, Tammy put her hands on my chest and gave me a small shove. "Don't, Luke."

"Tell me you didn't enjoy it," I said hoarsely. "Tell me it doesn't feel good, and I'll stop."

She couldn't say it—not honestly. So I kissed her again, and then I scooped her up in my arms and carried her to the bedroom. I poured my love into her that night, trying to make up for every tear, every sorrow I'd ever caused her. Afterward, we lay in each other's arms, completely wrecked.

"Well," Tammy said when she finally caught her breath, "you got your roll in the hay, Luke. I guess it's time for you to leave now, right?"

The words hurt me, though I knew I deserved them. "Please

don't be like that, Tammy," I said softly in the twilight. "This time I want to stay with you. Forever."

She looked beautiful the next morning, with the sun shining in the windows and playing off her hair. I tried to take her in my arms and kiss her, but she turned away from my kiss.

"I want you to go, Luke—before Tyler gets home."

"Why?"

"Because I don't want him to get the wrong idea."

I stared at her. "What's the right idea, then?"

"This was a mistake," she said, climbing out of bed. "It won't happen again."

"You can't mean that, Tammy. Not after last night."

"Especially after last night. I don't want you in my life anymore, Luke. Can't you understand that?"

I looked into her eyes and saw that she meant it—every word. I nearly choked on my disappointment. "Can I still see Tyler?"

"You can see him, but you're to meet him out on the front porch from now on. I don't want you in this house."

It was a tough pill to swallow, but I knew I had to play by her rules if I wanted to stay in the game.

As the next few weeks passed, Tammy stuck to the plan. Tyler would be waiting on the porch when I came to pick him up. When our visit was over, I'd knock on the door and Tammy would come to the window so I'd know she was home and it was okay to leave Tyler. I hated having to look at her through two panes of glass; it reminded me of the rare occasions in prison when I'd had visitors. Seeing Tammy from a distance was like a different kind of prison, but it was better than not seeing her at all.

Then one Sunday afternoon, Tyler and I were playing a game of catch in the park and we got rained out, so I took him home early. Back at Tammy's place, I knocked on the front door, but Tammy didn't come to the window. Still, her car was in the driveway, so I knew she must be home. After knocking a few more times, I finally went inside. After a quick check of the house, I decided that she must be in the shower, so I knocked on the bathroom door.

"Tyler's home," I called.

"Okay," came her muffled reply.

I waited a few minutes, but she didn't come out. Then I pressed my ear against the door. When I heard Tammy throwing up in there, I pushed the door open and stuck my head in. Tammy was crouched beside the toilet, and definitely not happy to see me.

"Get out of here, Luke."

"Are you okay?"

"Do I look okay?"

"If you have the flu or something, I can stay and hang out with Tyler for a while if you want to lay down and rest."

"I don't have the flu." To my surprise, she burst into tears. "I'm pregnant!"

I felt like I'd been hit between the eyes with a hammer. "What did you say?"

"You heard me!"

"Was—is it Neil's?"

She choked back a sob, and then she looked at me angrily and cried, "It's yours!"

I went to her and dropped to my knees beside her. "Tammy . . . I—I don't know what to say."

She started crying even harder then. "You don't have to say anything, Luke, because I'm not having this baby!"

"Please, Tammy—don't say that—"

"What else can I say? I don't want to abort this baby, but I can't raise two children alone, and after all you've put me through, how can I possibly make a life with you now?"

I knew that she was right. But I also knew that I couldn't let her throw us away. Not when I'd come to love her so much.

"You've got a few weeks yet before you have to decide anything. I'm begging you, Tammy. Please. Just think about it."

I didn't sleep at all that night. I was a mixed-up mess of emotions—joy, sorrow, and fear . . . but at least I knew one thing for certain: This was my last chance to make something of my life.

The next morning, I drove over to Tammy's house, determined to make her hear me out. "I missed the boat last time," I told her plainly, from the bottom of my heart. "I don't want to miss it again, Tammy. I want our baby, and I want Tyler, and I want us. And I'm going to be here, Tammy, for all of it. Just give me another chance. I swear to you—you won't ever be sorry again."

She looked at me for a long time. I could see that she wanted to believe me, that some small part of her still loved me. But she wasn't that sweet, trusting girl I'd met seven years before. And that had everything to do with me—with all that I had done to—and hadn't done for—her and Tyler.

And so I worked hard to earn back Tammy's trust and her respect. I honestly don't think I've ever worked so hard for anything in my life, but then, there's never been anything I wanted more than this.

Two months ago, I married Tammy for the second time. Tonight, I'm writing all of this down because I can't sleep, and I don't want to toss and turn and wake Tammy. She's going to need her strength, because tomorrow, she's scheduled to go in for a

C-section. They tell us it's going to be another boy.

Earlier, I was lying beside her in our bed tonight, thinking about promises, and about second chances, and about a lifetime of things that I want to do for and share with my awesome wife and sons. I thank God every day now for giving them back to me, and I pray that He'll give me the strength to be the man I need to be to raise our children right.

I don't want to waste one precious second of our forever, because if there's one thing I've learned, it's that little boys grow up. And sometimes—

So do grown men.

THE END

THE PRODIGAL WIFE
Can my husband ever forgive me for being
such a desperate, delusional fool?

"Lana, can I have a word with you, please?"

I looked up from the display of greeting cards I was
restocking. My boss, Mr. Peete, stood behind the pharmacy
counter with a very grumpy look on his face.

Oh, Lord, what now? I thought, walking to the back of the
store. Is my cash drawer short again?

"What's up, Mr. Peete?"

"Sarah just called in sick. Is there any chance you can stay
until ten o'clock tonight?"

I didn't really want to stay. Some friends of mine were
throwing a party and I was looking forward to getting out early,
getting blotto, and just having a real, old-fashioned good time. But
I'd only recently been hired as a temporary clerk at the drugstore
and I was hoping to be kept on after the holiday rush ended.
And besides that—my twenty-five-hours-a-week paychecks barely
covered the rent on my furnished room, let alone the secretarial
course I was saving up to take.

Do the responsible thing, Lana, I told myself sternly.

"Sure, Mr. Peete," I said with a smile. "No problem."

I went back to my display not realizing that that simple
decision probably changed my life. If I hadn't stayed late that
night, I might never have met Burke, and then I don't know what
road my life would've led me down. All I can say is that I guess
my lucky stars were shining down on me that night, because they
brought such a wonderful man into my life.

It was three weeks before Christmas. A light, fluffy snow was
falling from the sky, making the old, run-down neighborhood look
soft and pretty. There was Christmas music playing on the store
sound system and I was humming along to "Holly Jolly Christmas"
as sung by Burl Ives, trying to get myself into the holiday mood.
I'd finished filling the greeting card racks and was opening the new
shipment of gift wrap that'd arrived that afternoon when the front
door opened and two men walked in. One of them was old—maybe
seventy—with a big voice and a heavy way of walking. The other
guy looked to be about twenty-five or -six.

I said hello to them and then continued working on my display. As I was refilling my bins, the old guy came up behind me, nearly scaring me out of my skin.

"I'm gonna buy a present for Alice," he announced loudly.

I took a good look at him and realized he was mentally retarded. "That's nice," I said.

"Alice is my girlfriend."

I took a tiny step away from him. "Well, it's nice of you to buy your girlfriend a present."

He was still standing much too close for comfort, but he didn't seem to notice that his nearness was creeping me out. I took another small step back, but he merely stepped in closer and jerked his thumb in the other guy's direction.

"Burke don't have no girlfriend no more, on account of Kerri dumped him."

I looked at the other guy, noticing for the first time that he had beautiful, gray eyes.

"Come on, Hubie," he said, looking more than a little embarrassed. "The lady has work to do and we have to find that present."

The old man smiled at me and then gave me a small wave before he turned and stomped away. I couldn't seem to keep myself from watching them as they walked up and down the aisles. The old man looked at everything in the store, talking nonstop, while the guy he called Burke answered his questions. Burke seemed to possess an endless supply of patience and he treated the old man with the utmost respect. He wasn't anything you'd see on the cover of a magazine—not by any stretch. In fact, he was kind of on the short side for a guy—maybe five-feet-five, tops—with unruly, blond curls that sprang out from underneath his wool cap. But I hadn't seen a lot of kindness in my eighteen years of life, and there was something I found totally sexy about his compassion for that elderly retarded man.

After they'd looked around for about an hour, they finally brought their purchases up to the register. The old man proudly placed his items on the counter.

"I've got twenty-five cards," he said, holding up a boxed set of glittery Christmas greeting cards. "I'm going to send them all to Alice."

"Maybe you can just send Alice the prettiest one, Hubie," Burke gently suggested. "After all, you've got a lot of other people on your list."

"Nope," the old man insisted, firmly shaking his head. "I'm gonna send them all to Alice."

110

"Well, we'll see." Burke winked at me over the old man's head and I hid a smile as I totaled the bill.

"These sure are pretty," Hubie said, running his hands over the sparkly cards.

"Yes, they are," I said. "Alice is a lucky lady."

"Alice is pretty, too." He peered at me. "But not as pretty as you."

I blushed. "Well, thank you. That will be twelve dollars and fifty-eight cents."

He turned to Burke. "She's pretty, Burkey. You should take her out on a date."

Burke actually blushed. "Yeah, I should do that. Why don't you get your wallet out, Hubie, and pay the lady so we can go home? You're supposed to be in bed at nine o'clock, remember?"

Ignoring him, the old man peered at my nametag. "L-A-N-A. That's Llama."

"It's Lana, Hubie," Burke corrected.

"You should take Llama out on a date since Kerri won't go out with you no more."

Burke colored slightly, looking embarrassed. "Hubie, that's private."

"Well she won't. And neither will Suzy. You said Suzy won't even give you the time of day."

"Thank you, Hubie," Burke muttered. He looked so embarrassed that I couldn't help smiling at him. I think I started to fall in love with him right then, at that exact moment.

I gave the old man his change, bagged up his purchases, and watched out the window as they drove away. "Come on back any time, Burke," I whispered. "I'll sure give you the time of day. In fact, I'll give you anything you want."

I know that sounds immoral, but I really didn't know any better. I knew what boys wanted and I'd learned a long time before that giving it to them was better than staying at home on a Saturday night with my mother and the parade of drunks that were constantly stumbling in and out of our trailer.

This isn't a high school boy, Lana, I immediately corrected myself. This is a man—twenty-five years old at least—and he's obviously got something wrong with him because why else would he be hanging out with some old retarded guy on a Saturday night?

But somehow, I couldn't stop thinking about Burke's sexy, gray eyes. He was obviously a nice guy—I'd seen that for myself. I couldn't help wondering what reasons a girl would have for dumping him.

For the next few days I watched the door constantly, hoping Burke would come into the drugstore again. But he didn't.

After the first of the year I got laid off from Peete's and took a job working as a counter girl at Sloppy Joe's, a burger place a few blocks from where I lived. I settled into my new job and tried to forget about Burke, telling myself that he was too old for me and that I'd probably never see him again, anyway. That's why I was totally surprised—and more than just a little bit happy—one Friday night when the front door of Sloppy Joe's opened and the old man walked in. He stomped up to the counter and stared at me and then he gave me a grin as big and wide as a city bus.

"I know you! You're Llama!"

I grinned, blushing a little at his exuberant loudness. "Hi, Hubie."

"How come you're working here now?"

"Because they've got killer chicken wings. Where's Burke tonight?"

"He's outside, trying to get Brenda out of the van."

A few minutes later the door opened again and Burke walked in with a girl who looked to be about my age, who had Down syndrome.

"Look, Burkey!" Hubie hollered. "I found Llama!"

Burke gave me a smile that actually made me quiver before coaxing the girl up to the counter. She was as quiet as Hubie was loud, and she ordered a fish sandwich and French fries without looking me in the eye. When I put her order on a tray, she pulled a crumpled one-dollar bill out of her pocket and carefully set it on the counter.

"No, sweetheart, that's a one-dollar bill," Burke told her patiently. "Try again."

The girl dug a five out of her pocket and showed it to him.

"Good job," he said. Then he turned to me and explained, "Brenda's learning how to manage her money."

"Good for you, Brenda," I encouraged. "Maybe when you figure it out, you can help me!"

"She don't catch on too quick, Llama," Hubie boomed.

"Hubie," Burke said warningly, "be nice."

The old man looked at me and shrugged.

Burke carried their tray over to a booth and they all sat down to eat. I watched them as I worked. By then, I realized that Burke worked at one of the group homes in town. Watching him with Hubie and Brenda, it was obvious that they were more than just a paycheck to him—that Burke really cared about them.

He's too old for you, Lana, I reminded myself. It's never going to happen so just get him out of your head.

Well, that was easier said than done. I just could not seem to stop thinking about Burke, and four nights later when he showed up at Sloppy Joe's alone, I found out that I'd been on his mind, too.

"Hey, Burke," I said. "Where's Hubie tonight?"

"Oh, I'm guessing he's at home, giving someone else a rough time—for a change," he said with a grin. "This is my night off."

I rang up his order—a dozen atomic wings and a bottle of Bud—and handed him his change.

"How do you like working at Sloppy Joe's?" he asked, pocketing the coins.

I shrugged. "I don't know. It pays the rent. Barely."

"Yeah," he said with an easy laugh, "I'm with you there."

We made small talk until his order came up. I arranged it on a tray along with a burger and fries for myself. "I was just about to go on my break," I said. "Mind if I sit with you?"

He looked a bit surprised but he said, "I'd like that, Lana."

We slid into a booth and started to talk. Burke gave me the same patient attention I'd seen him show Hubie and Brenda. That's another thing that made me love him; it wasn't very often that I could talk to someone and feel that they really cared about what I had to say, but Burke really listened to me. He paid attention.

We talked for about thirty-five minutes. Then my break was over, but no way was I going to let Burke get away without making darned sure I'd see him again, so I gave him my sultriest smile and said, "It's been great talking with you, Burke. We should go out sometime. We could see a movie . . . or something."

He didn't answer right away. Then finally, he asked, "How old are you, Lana?"

"I'm eighteen. How old are you?"

He chuckled. "About ten years too old to be thinking what I'm thinking."

"I'm not a little girl, Burke," I protested.

"I can see that, sweetheart."

I knew then and there that Burke was as interested as I was, but also that he was the kind of guy who plays by the rules. He didn't want to get involved with me because of our age difference, but having him back away from me only made me want him more. I learned from my mother at a young age how to manipulate men and get what I want from them, so I quickly changed my tactics.

"I like talking to you, Burke," I said. "I know there are too many years between us for a romance. What I really need is a friend."

He thought about that for a minute. "Okay," he said.

Since we both worked evenings we made a date for the next afternoon. All in all it was the perfect friendship date, and Burke acted like the perfect gentleman. He took me to a place called The Winter Garden, an ice skating rink surrounded by evergreens decorated with soft, white lights and shiny, red bows. Pretty love songs and Golden Oldies played over the P.A. system and although I'd never been ice-skating before, I caught on pretty fast. We spent the entire afternoon laughing like a couple of kids, skating round and round in our winter wonderland.

Afterward, we walked to a nearby doughnut shop and drank hot chocolate and talked over glazed and jelly-filled doughnuts. We talked about Sloppy Joe's and the secretarial course I wanted to take, and then Burke told me about the ARC group home where he'd worked for the past eight years.

"It's not great money, but I love the work," he said. "And the residents are the best. They don't know how to be anything but honest, which I find to be pretty refreshing."

"I don't know if I could work with them," I admitted, blushing. "Actually, retarded people have always sort of weirded me out—until I met Hubie and Brenda, that is."

"That's why we like to get them out in the community. If we can expose them to society, then maybe we can build understanding and tolerance." He drank the last of his hot chocolate and set his mug down on the table. "If you ever have any spare time, you should come by the house. They'd love the company."

"Can I ask you a personal question, Burke?"

He smiled. "I guess that depends on what it is."

"What happened with you and Kerri?"

He took a long time answering. "She wanted things I couldn't afford to give her, Lana," he finally said. "Kerri's a material girl, and—what can I say? I'm a simple guy."

I was definitely not a simple girl. No, far from it, in fact. Having grown up with nothing, I craved things like nice clothes, expensive jewelry, and a Ford Mustang convertible. But I knew even then that I'd have to adjust my way of thinking if I wanted to be with Burke.

Over the next few weeks we spent a lot of time together. We went skating at The Winter Garden and to matinees at the Star Theater. Sometimes we just ordered a pizza and hung out at Burke's apartment, talking and putting together jigsaw puzzles or watching cheesy movies on cable. I had a lot of leftover issues from my childhood and I found myself sharing them with Burke. He was better than any therapist I could've hired.

I also started dropping by the group home whenever I had a night off. I'd play checkers with Hubie or paint Brenda's fingernails and after a few visits, Brenda could actually look me in the eye when she spoke to me and her face would light up as soon as I walked in the door. I really enjoyed spending time at the home and the residents treated me like I was royalty. Mostly, I liked watching Burke work with them; I loved his kindness and his gentle spirit. I'd been out with a lot of guys and usually had sex on the first or second date, but Burke stuck to our agreement: He was the best friend I ever had.

Meanwhile, I wanted him so badly that it hurt.

It was the middle of March before I got an opportunity to act on those feelings.

It was a Saturday morning. We'd had a big snowstorm in the night and Burke called me and invited me to go tubing at Chestnut Ridge, the local ski resort. I'd never done that before, either, but Burke was always encouraging me to try new things.

After a fun-filled day we went back to his apartment. The heavy storm had knocked out the power, so we lit candles. It was so romantic—wrapped up in a warm cocoon of blankets with Burke's battery-operated radio playing softly while the snow piled up outside. Burke looked totally sexy with his wind-burned cheeks and his gray eyes glittering in the candlelight, and I told him so.

He chuckled. "Me? Sexy? Come on, Lana."

"I mean it. There's something special about you, Burke. The way you listen. The way you care about people. The residents at the group home are totally in love with you." I dropped my voice to a whisper. "And so am I."

We kissed, and suddenly I felt like I was wrapped in a blanket of fire. But Burke pulled away from me.

"Lana . . . I'm not sure this is a good idea. . . ."

"I just want to make you feel as good as you make me feel, Burke." I wrapped my arms around him and pressed my body close to his. "It's okay if you don't feel the same way."

"If I don't feel the same way?" He pulled away and stared into my eyes. "Lana, I'm so far gone on you that I'll probably never make it back. So if you're just playing—if this isn't real—then you need to tell me now, before it goes too far."

It was real. I told him so—but not with words. I told him so with every part of me, and in every way that I knew how. When it was over, I actually cried tears of joy.

The next day my skin still burned from his touch and my head was filled with the sweet words he'd said to me. I was euphoric; I was in love. I was also terrified. After all, I'd seen how much my mom loved my dad. I'd also seen what a mess she turned into after he walked out on us. I'd promised myself a long time ago that no man would ever have that kind of chokehold on me.

That night, when Burke came into Sloppy Joe's during my dinner break, my heart squeezed in my chest at the sight of him.

Don't let him win, I cautioned myself. Don't let him own you.

We sat across from each other in our usual booth and he took both of my hands in his. "I can't stop thinking about you, Lana," he said. "I've been going crazy all day, wondering what you're doing and when I can be with you again."

"You're with me now," I teased, grinning to make light of the moment, though it was anything but, considering Burke's old-fashioned earnestness.

He smiled indulgently. "That's not really what I meant, Lana. What time do you get out of here tonight?"

"I have to stay and close."

"Can I pick you up afterward?"

I really wanted to be with him that night, but somehow, I wasn't seeing his face then, or even hearing his voice. All I could hear was my mother's voice in my head, screaming that men are no better than animals, that all they really want is to control, to own. And though deep down I knew that wasn't true about Burke, a mean little part of me wanted to hurt him, anyway.

"I can't see you tonight, Burke," I said. "I have plans to go to a party."

"Oh." He was trying not to show his disappointment, and failing badly. "How about tomorrow, then?"

"Yeah, okay. Tomorrow."

"Great," he said with a smile that didn't quite reach his eyes. "I'll call you in the morning."

I watched him walk out of the restaurant, a smug smile on my face. I told myself I'd won. But for the rest of that night I couldn't stop seeing the look in Burke's eyes when I shot him down.

After work I went to the party, but I had a miserable time. Burke was on my mind. I drank too much beer and danced with too many guys and when one of them started to grope me, it made me feel sick to my stomach. I left the party and walked across town to Burke's apartment, frozen to the bone and crying all the way.

He answered the door in his bathrobe. "Lana? What are you doing here?"

"I—I want to be with you, Burke," I blubbered.

"Baby, it's two o'clock in the morning." He peered at me in the darkness. "Are you drunk?"

"N-no," I said, my teeth chattering. "Well—maybe just a little bit."

"Come inside; you're frozen." He led me to the couch and wrapped me in a blanket.

"I—I wanted to be with you, Burke—the whole time!" I sobbed. "I didn't even want to go to that lame-o party!"

"Why did you, then?"

"I don't know!" I wailed.

"Come here." He wrapped his arms around me. "Don't cry, Lana. It's no big deal."

"But it is a big deal! I hurt you on purpose and I don't even know why!"

He stroked my hair, soothing me like I was a child. "Shhh."

"Burke," I whispered, "I said I love you, but that's not quite true. The truth is, I—I don't think I know how to love."

He pulled me closer. "I don't think I know how not to. I don't want to smother you, Lana, but when I feel something this strongly, my instinct is to run with it."

"And mine is to run away," I sniffled. "So? How do we make this work, then?"

"We learn how to crawl, baby."

That didn't really make sense to me at the time, but I liked that he had a solution to our problem. A few weeks later, I moved into Burke's apartment. It was small, with only one bedroom, but compared to my rented room it was a palace. Burke wouldn't let me help out with the bills, insisting that I take my money and enroll in my secretarial course, instead. Burke dreamed of having a son someday, but I had an ectopic pregnancy when I was fifteen and my fallopian tubes were badly scarred as a result. But even knowing that I couldn't give him a child, Burke still wanted me. Burke was a loving, giving man and I was the selfish little girl who didn't even begin to deserve him. I didn't believe in marriage or in making a lifelong commitment to anyone, but for Burke, just living together wasn't enough. I was scared, but deep down I wanted to be taken care of and I knew that Burke would die for me if he had to. We got married the following year when I was nineteen and he was twenty-nine.

The first five years of our marriage were the happiest of my life. I took my secretarial course and then got a job working as a part-time receptionist at the hospital. I made new friends and I learned how to cook and keep house. Burke transferred to the dayshift so we could have our evenings together, and we even started looking into adopting a child.

Burke would've probably been content to stay in our little

apartment forever, but after awhile the walls seemed to close in around me. My friends at the hospital were a different class of people than I was used to hanging out with and I'd go to their beautiful houses and come back to our apartment feeling utterly depressed. I wanted to have all of the nice things that they had, even though I knew darn well that Burke and I couldn't afford any of it. Nonetheless, I convinced Burke to start looking at houses with me, telling him that when the time came for us to adopt a baby, we'd need another bedroom for a nursery.

Well, we looked at what seemed like a hundred homes and we couldn't qualify for a mortgage on any of them. After a few months I started to feel downright desperate to have a home of my own, and then one Sunday morning I saw a job advertisement in the Classifieds and nearly jumped for joy.

"Look at this, Burke," I said, handing the paper across the table to him. "Larchmont Electronics is opening up a new plant right here in town. They're hiring fifty people and all you need is a high school diploma. Just look what the starting pay is!"

He glanced at the ad, and then at me. "What are you thinking?"

"I'm thinking that if I got that job, combined with what you make, we'd be able to get a loan with no problem."

"I don't want you working in a factory, Lana."

"Why not?"

"Because it's rough work and probably not the greatest atmosphere." He went back to his Sports section like that was the end of the discussion.

"I don't mind hard work. And the 'atmosphere' can't be any worse than the one I grew up in."

"Lana, honey, you need to be patient. We'll save some more money and then in a couple of years—"

"Years? But I want a house now, Burke!"

"This place isn't so bad, is it?"

"Are you kidding? It's terrible! I hate it."

Burke and I didn't have many fights, but we had one that day. We ended up shouting at each other and I said some very unkind things. When I was finished with my tirade, he glared at me.

"Hey, if I'm not enough for you, baby, then by all means—there's the door!"

I got up from the table, too stunned to speak, and walked out, slamming the door shut behind me so hard that I broke a pane of glass.

A week later I came home from work to find Burke dressed in his good clothes. "Why are you all dressed up?" I asked him.

"I interviewed for a job with Larchmont Electronics this afternoon."

My heart nearly stopped beating. "You did?"

He nodded curtly. "I start next week on the four-to-midnight shift."

"But—but, Burke—you mean you'd leave ARC? You'd do that—for me?"

"There's nothing I wouldn't do for you, Lana."

And so Burke traded a job he loved for my happiness.

After a few months of looking, we finally found a three-bedroom brick house on a pretty street called October Lane. The house was plain compared to its gorgeous neighbors, but to me, it looked like a mansion. Burke went to talk to our loan officer the very next day.

"We qualify for the house, Lana," he told me that night over our dinner of chicken tetrazzini, "but with property taxes being what they are, the mortgage is going to be a nightmare. We'd have to be really careful about our spending."

"I will be," I said quickly.

He looked at me pointedly. "There won't be money for any extras. Are you really sure this is what you want, babe?"

"I've never wanted anything more."

Two months later we moved into the house on October Lane.

At first, I was in heaven. Burke and I painted every room and I even took a class to learn how to stencil the walls. Burke and his brothers put on a new roof and we added a small porch onto the back that overlooked our beautiful garden with the goldfish pond. I occupied the long evenings while Burke was at work with decorating my new house and I was the happiest woman alive.

Then the house was finally finished, finally complete—and I was the loneliest.

All of my new friends had husbands and kids so I really didn't have anyone to socialize with. Night after night I sat alone in my lovely house, wondering if it was worth it. I was so bored and lonely at times that I felt like I could die.

And then I met Eli.

I really don't know how it happened. I certainly never set out to cheat on Burke. The best way I can describe it is to say that some people only want what they can't have. And I guess I was one of those people.

I'd been employed by the hospital for almost five years by the time Eli got hired as a janitor. He came into my office one afternoon to empty the wastebaskets and I noticed he had a killer backside and a smile that turned me into a quivering mass of jelly.

That first day he hung around for a long time after he'd collected the trash and we talked about the hospital and about the different jobs we'd had. Eli had had a lot of them, it turned out. Even then, I got the feeling that maybe he wasn't very responsible, but I thoroughly enjoyed his quirky sense of humor and easygoing way.

After that, Eli came into my office every day and stayed a little bit longer each time. His visits quickly became the highpoints of my days, for Eli Nash was sexy and fun to talk to. He was twenty-two years old—three years younger than I, and thirteen years younger than Burke. I never thought the age difference between Burke and me was a big deal . . . until I met Eli.

They met each other briefly one afternoon when Burke dropped by the hospital to take me out to lunch. The next day, when Eli came in to empty the wastebaskets, he gave me his sexy, dimpled smile.

"So tell me, Lana—what's a little hottie like you doing with that old dude?"

"Burke's not old," I said defensively. "He's only thirty-five."

"He looks about fifty."

"He does not!"

I pretended to be insulted, but after Eli said that, I started to notice the tiny laugh lines around Burke's eyes and the spot on the top of his head where his hair was starting to thin.

Eli and I started having dinner together a couple of nights a week in the hospital cafeteria. I knew Burke wouldn't like it, and I actually twisted it all around in my head and made it all Burke's fault, for taking an evening shift. After all, why should I eat dinner alone every night? I told myself that the dinners were perfectly innocent. I told myself it was no big deal. And it really wasn't a big deal—until the night Eli invited me to go out to a bar after dinner.

"A hottie like you shouldn't be sitting home all alone every night," he said. "Come to Shenanigans with me and my friends. We'll show you a good time."

At first I said no. But then I started to remember the good old days—back when I used to party and dance all night long. Then I started meeting Eli and his friends at Shenanigans one night a week. And then gradually, one night a week turned into three nights a week, and then five nights a week.

As it was, everything about Burke started to annoy me. I hated the country music he listened to, and the way he sang along with it at the top of his lungs in the shower, even though he can't carry a tune to save his life. I hated the way he scoured the checkbook if our bank balance was even so much as a penny off, and I hated the way he always patiently explained things to me just as if he was back at the group home and I was one of his charges. I even began to hate the way he made love to me.

I begged him to take me out dancing, but Burke was always too tired and on his nights off, he always wanted to go and visit the group home or stay at home and rent movies—activities I used to enjoy which now seemed like colossal bores. I wanted to go out and party with my new friends. I wanted to have fun. Indeed, I started to dread Burke's nights off because they meant that I couldn't be with Eli. And from the dance floor in Shenanigans, it was only a hop, skip, and a jump into Eli's waterbed.

After a few months, Eli started putting pressure on me to leave Burke. He even went so far as to make an appointment for me with a divorce lawyer.

"Just go and talk to the guy, Lana," he urged. "What can it hurt?"

"I'm afraid to, Eli. I don't know if I'm ready to take that step yet."

"Do what you've gotta do then, baby, but I'm not gonna wait around forever."

I looked into his eyes and saw that he meant it.

It was time for me to choose.

In the weeks while I waited for my appointment, I tried at least a hundred times to tell Burke about my affair with Eli, but knowing how badly it would hurt him, I just couldn't do it.

As it was, Burke seemed to sense how unhappy I'd become, and he actually took me to Vermont for a romantic, three-day weekend even though we really couldn't afford it. We stayed at a cozy, little bed-and-breakfast and spent the weekend horseback riding, hiking, and shopping in the antique stores. We talked a lot about our marriage and how to make it better and I started remembering all of the things that I did love about Burke and I even promised myself that I'd break it off with Eli. But when I was back home and back in Eli's arms, my resolve melted like a snowball in the sun.

On the day before my appointment, I called the law office a dozen times, hanging up each time before the call went through. My stomach hurt so badly that I couldn't keep food down; I couldn't keep my mind on my work and I was so relieved when four o'clock came at last.

Later, as soon as I turned onto October Lane and saw Burke's truck sitting in our driveway, I knew something bad was going to happen. For one thing, it wasn't Burke's day off, and for another, in more than six years of marriage I'd never known Burke to be sick. So whatever his reasons were for being home at four-fifteen on a Thursday afternoon, I knew they probably weren't good. I pulled in beside his truck and took a few minutes to compose myself before I went inside.

Burke was sitting on the couch, watching TV and drinking a beer. There were three empty beer bottles on the coffee table and the sight of them really made my stomach ache. Burke never drank more than two beers; moreover, he never drank in the middle of the afternoon.

"Why aren't you at work?" I asked nervously.

He turned off the TV, took a swallow of beer, and set the empty bottle beside the others. "You got a call from Jim Henson's office this morning. They wanted to confirm your appointment for tomorrow afternoon."

I felt myself grow numb. Burke just stared at me, waiting for an explanation, but I couldn't bring myself to give him one. Instead, I turned and walked into the kitchen.

Burke followed, watching from the doorway as I put a filter into the coffee maker and filled it with freshly ground coffee from Starbucks. "Do you want to tell me what's going on?" he asked.

"I'm seeing a lawyer, Burke," I said, trying to keep my voice steady. "I want out."

"You can't be serious, Lana."

"I'm not happy, Burke. I told you that in Vermont."

"Yes, and I thought we agreed that we were going to work on our relationship."

"We don't have a relationship!" I shouted, turning to glare at him. "We never even see each other anymore!"

"And why is that, Lana?" he shouted back. "Do you think you can answer that for me?"

I lowered my eyes, too ashamed to answer.

"Correct me if I'm wrong, Lana, but I think I took this lousy job so I could afford to buy you this house. And now you want out? Is that what this marriage has been all about, Lana—just a clever way for you to get a mortgage?"

"Of course not!"

"Lana . . . baby." He was trying desperately to calm down. He came over to where I stood and wrapped his arms around me. "Things aren't that bad, are they? Not so bad that we can't work them out."

"This marriage was about me having someone to share my life with, Burke. But you're not that person anymore." I swallowed the tears I felt coming. "I don't love you anymore, Burke."

I might as well have shot him for all of the pain I saw then in his gray, weary eyes. "You can't mean that."

"I do mean it."

122

He stared into my eyes, trying hard to understand. "Is there someone else?"

I looked away.

"Jeez, Lana." When I looked at him again, I saw tears flooding his eyes. "There's someone else?"

I nodded once. "I'm sorry," I whispered.

"When were you going to tell me all of this?"

I didn't have an answer for that. Up until ten minutes before I wasn't even sure I was going to go through with the law appointment. "I don't know."

He started to cry—so hard that it scared me.

"Burke, I'm so sorry."

"How could you do this?" he howled like a man on the very brink of despair.

I couldn't answer him. All I could do was stand there and watch him cry.

Finally Burke turned and walked out, slamming the door shut behind him. By then I was used to being in the house alone, but that was a completely different kind of alone—it was the cold, empty kind that said that Burke was never coming back.

Well, Lana, it's over, I told myself. This is what you wanted. You should be glad.

But instead of relief, all I felt was sorrow.

The next day the lawyer drew up a separation agreement. As it was, on my salary, I couldn't afford to make the mortgage payments on the house and Burke didn't want it, so we finally agreed to put it up for sale. We decided that Burke would live in the house until it sold, and the day after Burke signed the separation agreement, I moved into Eli's apartment.

Soon, my life was filled with partying and dancing, and sex. Eli was much more adventurous in bed than Burke was, but I have to admit that he wasn't anywhere near as sincere. After our lovemaking, Eli usually passed out. Then I'd roll over and cry into my pillow, thinking of Burke and how he used to hold me all night long like I was his very own precious treasure.

To make matters worse, Eli had a lot of other nasty little habits that I guess I never wanted to see before. He was a disgusting slob to live with and he definitely expected me to pick up after him and more or less wait on him hand and foot. He was also moody and selfish and worst of all—he started to put me down a lot, belittling me until I was often reduced to tears. He'd always laugh once I started crying and insist that he was only kidding, but I got the feeling that he really enjoyed hurting me in some sick way. A month after my separation from Burke I sat in the cruddy, little bathroom of Eli's apartment, crying my eyes out, knowing I'd made a terrible mistake.

Indeed, it wasn't long before I actually started to feel physically ill. My stomach ached and my head felt foggy all the time as I grew more and more depressed while Eli grew meaner and meaner. I thought of Burke constantly, remembering all of the little things—like skating at The Winter Garden and all of the Christmas trees we'd decorated together through our marriage. I thought of the way he always got up early to make my coffee and bring it to me in bed. As it was, I now spent many of my days hungover with Eli criticizing me for not knowing how to "handle" my liquor. I couldn't stop remembering how Burke used to make me dry toast when I was sick and rub my back until I fell asleep. All along I was the one who'd had a treasure. And I didn't even know it.

Needless to say, after a few months of wild living I started missing a lot of time at work and I was actually close to getting fired, so I vowed to stop drinking and going out at night. Then I sat in the apartment alone at night while Eli went out with his friends till five and six in the morning. After awhile I started to get the distinct feeling that he was cheating on me.

"What do you expect, baby?" he asked me when I confronted him. "These days, you're about as much fun as a flat tire!"

So in order to make Eli happy, I went back to being a party animal.

One night after work we went out to a bar called The Sidewinder for pizza and chicken wings. As soon as we pulled into the parking lot, I recognized Burke's truck parked in the rear.

"We can't go in, Eli," I said immediately.

"Why not?" he asked snappishly. "Now what's the problem?"

"Burke's here."

"So?"

"So, I don't want to rub his nose in it."

"I do," he said with a smirk.

He wrapped his arm around my shoulders and walked me in acting more loud and obnoxious than I'd ever seen him before. Almost immediately, Burke looked up from the bar, where he'd been eating his dinner. Our eyes locked and I could see in his just how sad he was and how much I'd hurt him. Then Eli hustled me out back to the pool table and when I looked again, Burke was gone.

My instinct was to rush out to the parking lot and get in his truck with him. Oh, how I ached to go home—to pop some popcorn, turn on the TV, and sit on the couch with my husband.

One morning a few days after that night, I ran into Tim Hortons to pick up a box of doughnuts for the girls at work. Once again, I stopped dead in my tracks when I saw Burke sitting at a table with a beautiful blonde. Tears flooded my eyes and I left the premises before Burke noticed me.

What did you expect, Lana? Did you think he was going to cry forever? Did you think other women would never notice how wonderful he is?

I sank deeper into depression until it became my constant companion, a darker presence than anything I'd ever known. I refused to go out and meanwhile, girls called the apartment constantly. I knew for certain then that Eli was fooling around on me—and I honestly didn't even care. In fact, I didn't care about anything. I stopped working out at the gym and I stopped wearing makeup. My looks went to sod until people who knew me stopped recognizing me for the pretty, bright thing I used to be.

In return, Eli started to hit me.

The year I spent living with Eli is the worst year of my life. I was so homesick that I wanted to die and when I thought of "home," it wasn't the house on October Lane I thought of, but Burke's arms. I was like a spoiled-rotten brat who ran away from home. The only difference was that I could never go back.

Then one evening, just as I was pretty much about to give up on life altogether, Burke called me out of the blue. "Good news, Lana," he said. "We got a purchase offer on the house."

"That's great news," I said, trying to squeeze some sincerity into my voice.

"Yeah. I'm starting to pack up, but there are some things here that I'm not sure about what to do with. I was thinking you might want some of the furniture, and you left behind some of your clothes. Actually, Lana, I was hoping you'd come over some time and help me sort through things."

Our year's separation was almost up. I knew that Burke would probably want the divorce to go through as quickly as possible, so a few days later I went to see my lawyer, and then I drove over to October Lane. I wore a heavy coat of makeup to cover the latest bruise Eli had put on my face, and a big, bulky sweater to try to hide the extra thirty pounds I'd gained. Walking up to the front door, I was filled with dread thinking that Burke might be entertaining his new girlfriend inside. It took every ounce of courage I possessed to ring the doorbell.

"Hi, Lana," Burke said, opening the door. "Thanks for coming."

I can't describe to you what it was like, walking back in

through that door. Burke had told me that he'd packed up some things, but I wasn't prepared for the emptiness—the loneliness—I sensed inside of that house.

"Would you like a soda?" Burke asked, breaking into my dismal thoughts.

"Sure."

He brought us each a ginger ale and we moved into the den. We sat down on the couch and talked, but within a matter of minutes, our polite conversation lapsed into an awkward silence.

Burke took a swallow of his soda. "How's Eli?"

"He's fine," I said, shifting uncomfortably.

Burke looked at my face, and then looked away. "Did he do that to you?"

"What do you mean?"

"Did he put those bruises on your face?"

I stared at my hands, not answering.

"Lana," he whispered, "why?"

I knew what he was asking. Not why Eli hit me, but why I'd leave a man who loved me so much for such a miserable excuse for a human being.

"I don't want to talk about it, Burke." My gaze traveled to his hands and I was surprised to see that he still wore his wedding ring. I had no right to ask, but I just had to know, so I gathered up my courage and blurted out, "I saw you out a while ago—in Tim Hortons. You were sitting with a pretty girl—a blonde."

He seemed to think about it for a moment and I felt my heart sinking. How many women is he seeing? I wondered miserably.

"That must've been Crystal."

"She's pretty."

"Yeah, she's a cute girl."

I felt tears threatening, so I quickly changed the subject. "Are you still working at Larchmont?"

"No, actually, I'm back at ARC. They opened a new group home a few weeks ago and offered me a position as supervisor." He drained his glass and set it on the coffee table. "So things are looking up for me."

The words cut through me like a knife because things definitely were not looking up for me. In fact, things had never looked bleaker. I took the divorce papers out of my bag and handed them to him.

"What are these?"

"I had my lawyer draw up the divorce papers. Look them over and if everything seems to be in order, you just have to sign them and have them notarized. You can keep everything that's left in the

126

house. Good-bye, Burke." I stood and walked out of my house for the last time.

Outside, a light rain was falling. I was crying so hard that I couldn't even get my key into the car door lock; I was still fumbling with it when I heard Burke say my name. Then I frantically jiggled the key, desperate to get the door open—to get away. But the next thing I knew, Burke's arms were around me, holding me tight.

"Lana, we're not doing this."

"Wh-what do you mean?"

"We're not getting divorced." He pulled me deeper into his arms. "I'm not going to let him hurt you any more. And I'm not going to stand by and let you keep on hurting yourself."

I was stunned. "But—what about your girlfriend?"

"Crystal's my therapist. She's been helping me to try to sort out my head, which has been a mess ever since you left." His voice broke. "Lana . . . it's time for you to come home."

All at once I was sobbing. "You—you'd take me back—after all of the awful things I've done to you—to us?"

"I love you, Lana. More than words can express."

"But—how can you still feel that way after I betrayed you—after I hurt you so? Oh, Burke—how can it ever be the same?"

"It won't ever be the same, Lana, but that doesn't mean that it can't be good. I don't know how it's possible; I just know that it is."

Burke and I have been back together for almost six months now. With the money from the sale of our house on October Lane we were able to make a down payment on a place on Cottage Street. The neighborhood is not as prestigious and the house is not as big, but it's the perfect house in which to start over. It needs a lot of work, but so does our marriage, and I know that with a lot of time and love and patience, both can be restored to their former beauty. Burke and I still have a lot of issues to work through, but I thank God every day for the love he still has for me, a love that refused to die.

The point of my story is that there are some things in life worth hanging onto, and a good marriage is one of them. I hope that if someone out there reads this and recognizes herself in me, she'll take my advice: If your marriage is not that bad . . . if you're just bored . . . please, please hang in there. Believe me when I say that it's the ordinary things you miss—the small, beautiful moments you take for granted that make life worth living.

They say that good marriages are made in heaven, and that may be true. But sometimes you have to walk through hell to get there.

As for Burke and me—

We're learning how to crawl.

THE END

WHEN MOMMY
HAS AN AFFAIR
Can a family survive?

As I pulled up outside my friend Lauren's apartment block, my mind was still on the chaos I'd just left behind. I wondered what new disorder might await me upon my return home.

My husband, Stephen, had barely looked up from the TV, but I had the feeling that as soon as he ate dinner he'd start yet another "home improvement" project. I wished with all my heart that he would finish just one of them. Our house looks like a war zone and I'm fed up with it.

Lauren ran down her front steps to my car and opened the door. "Hey! It's freezing, isn't it?"

"You'll be warm soon," I said, turning up the heater as she got in. "Are you nervous?"

"Terrified! But I can't let my divorce put me off men forever. And you sure are sweet to come out with me tonight."

Although it did seem wrong for me to be doing it, I said, "I guess I'd be a little scared, too, if I were getting back into the dating game."

But secretly, I have to admit to you that it was liberating to be out. Stephen never took me anywhere and lately, I'd started to feel like my life consisted of nothing but work, the kids, and the house.

The week prior, Lauren had told me that a new club in the next town over was advertising Ladies' Night on Friday nights. "You'll come with me a few times, won't you?" she asked. "My car's in the repair shop and, anyway, I'd hate to go alone."

"Of course," I replied. "I'm sure Stephen won't mind."

As I pulled into traffic, Lauren continued, "When I married Jonathan I thought it'd be forever. Who knew I'd waste five years of my life on that guy?"

"It wasn't all bad, was it?"

She sighed. "No, you're right. But the last eighteen months were complete and total hell, as you well know."

"Let's hope you meet someone ten times better than Jonathan."

The club was crowded. Lauren ordered drinks and I found a table against the back wall. As I looked around I saw that a lot of the women were wearing miniskirts no wider than belts, extremely low-cut blouses, tons of jewelry, and tons of makeup.

There are more exposed midriffs in here than there are on Galveston Beach in July, I mused.

Shrugging off my coat, I untied the wool scarf from around my neck and placed my gloves in my purse. My khakis and loose turtleneck sweater made me feel invisible, but immediately, I thought, That's okay. I'm not here to attract a man, after all—I'm just here to support Lauren, and that's all.

I met Lauren when I started working in the doctor's office where she's the manager, five years ago. I'm quiet by nature and I don't gossip much with the other staff, but Lauren also attends my yoga classes and we got to know each other there. I consider her a friend; in fact, at the time, she was my only friend.

Lauren returned with our drinks. "Lots of men," she said, grinning.

I grinned, too, happy for her. "See anyone you'd like to get to know?"

"There are several decent-looking guys." She sipped her margarita.

I lifted my ginger ale in a toast. "To a good start." We clinked glasses and smiled at each other.

"How's the decorating?" Lauren asked.

"Please. Don't get me started," I said, wishing she hadn't brought up the subject. "There're no cupboard doors in the kitchen and Stephen's decided he wants to "reposition" the fridge, which means he has to knock out the pantry." I didn't even bother telling her that our daughter, Emma, was still waiting for closet doors to be installed in her bedroom, that the baseboards in Ethan's room had been stripped but needed painting, and that the staircase still had six test patches of paint on one wall. Stephen and I had decided three months ago on Butterchurn, but the paint cans remained in our garage, unopened.

Lauren knew all about Stephen's attempts at do-it-yourself. "You're a saint to put up with the mess. I know I wouldn't stand for it."

I chewed my lip. I'm not a saint. The whole thing drove me crazy, but my tentative requests for Stephen to please finish one project before starting another fell on deaf ears. My mom drove my father away with her constant bitching when I was eight and I vowed never to turn into that kind of nagging, complaining harpy. However, I seemed to have gone in the opposite direction. Neither Stephen nor my children listened to me; they just did as they pleased. I honestly felt like my true self was squashed beneath a veneer of amenability, but I wasn't at all sure about how to get things back on track, so I continued to let things slide.

Two men came over and asked us to dance. I refused, politely, but Lauren accepted and followed her Stetson-wearing partner out onto the dance floor. As I sipped my soda I thought about the weekend ahead, planning meals and trying to remember what activities the kids were scheduled for. Then a voice interrupted my thoughts.

"Why are you over here all by yourself?"

I looked up at a tall, lean man wearing a blue, denim shirt that matched his eyes. I guess I looked surprised and he grinned.

"You were deep in thought," the man said, pulling out a chair and sitting down next to me. "Trying to fix the world?"

I laughed. "Just my small part of it."

"Like some company?"

"Why not?" I said, feeling unusually bold. "But. . . ."

"But what?"

"Well, I'm not actually here to find a partner. I'm just here for moral support. It's my friend who's single. I'm married."

The man nodded. "James." He held out his hand and I shook it.

"Hi, I'm Meadow."

"How about another drink, Meadow?"

"But I told you—"

"Yeah, that you're married; I haven't forgotten already, although it's my bad luck. However, I've been on my feet all day and I don't feel like dancing, so why don't we just keep each other company?" He pointed to my glass. "What're you drinking?"

"Ginger ale—I'm driving," I explained. "But I'd love another."

"Fine."

When James returned with our drinks I told him all about Lauren, hoping he'd let me introduce her to him. But he just glanced at my friend when I pointed her out and then turned his attention back to me.

"She looks like she won't have any trouble finding a date," he said. "Now, tell me about yourself. Do you work?"

I gave him an edited story of my life: husband, twelve-year-old Ethan and ten-year-old Emma, my job in medical insurance billing, and Stephen's job with a building supplies firm. James seemed genuinely interested, which was a novelty for me. Conversations with my husband were limited those days to, "Can you get me a beer?" or "Where's the TV remote?"

The talk moved on to current affairs and movies. Since I watch TV and rented movies in between ferrying my kids to their activities, I was able to hold up my end of the conversation. Then James told me that he'd been divorced for three years and had no children. He spent most weekends in the summer riding his Harley out in the country and he also liked fishing. When I asked him about his job he told me that he was a property developer.

"Really? You should speak to my husband," I joked.

"What do you mean?"

"When he isn't at work, Stephen's 'developing' our property."

James smiled. "Oh?"

I sighed. "We have this big, old house that we've been renovating for years."

Although I said "we," it was really all up to Stephen. He wouldn't let me help, always telling me that I don't know one end of a paintbrush from the other. I always told him that I was more than willing to learn, but he said he didn't have the time. Time; huh! He had plenty of time, but when he should've been getting on with the renovations, he was always out with his buddies and I'd be left sitting in the mess, fuming.

"It's a long story," I told James. "I'd rather talk about something else."

I finally relaxed and was actually enjoying myself when my cell phone rang. I fished it out of my purse.

"Mom?" It was my daughter.

"What's wrong, Emma?"

"I'm still at Lindsay's. Dad forgot to pick me up again and he doesn't answer the phone."

I glanced at my watch. It was almost eleven. Stephen had promised to put Emma's closet doors back on that night, so I wondered where he could be.

"Mom? Are you coming?"

"Yes, Em, I'm on my way."

James helped me on with my coat as I explained to him why I had to leave. "I hope everything's okay," he said.

"Thanks."

I wound my way through the tables and caught Lauren's eye. She whispered something in her partner's ear and came over to me. Her eyes were sparkling; I could see she was having a very good time.

I told her the problem.

"I understand," she said.

"Do you want me to come back for you?"

"No." She grinned naughtily. "I'll get a ride home."

"Be careful," I warned, sounding to myself like I was talking to Emma. "And call me tomorrow."

"I will."

Back at home, Emma and I entered the dark back hallway

and I tripped over Ethan's hockey bag. Cursing under my breath, I rubbed hard at my shin where the stick had caught me.

"Daddy forgot to replace the light bulb, didn't he?" Emma said.

"Yeah; if it wasn't so high up, I'd just do it myself."

We found Stephen washing his hands at the kitchen sink. "Hey, pumpkin. What's the matter?" he asked, seeing the scowl on Emma's face.

"You forgot me!" She stomped past him and helped herself to a glass of milk from the fridge.

"I was in the garage." He glanced at the phone on the counter. The red light blinked, showing three messages. "I never heard it ring."

"I'll bet you had the radio on loud, didn't you?" I asked, annoyance creeping into my tone. I could never rely on Stephen; as it was, I'd even cut my yoga classes down to one evening a week since he kept forgetting to pick up Ethan after choir practice.

Stephen threw me a sharp glance. "What's the big deal? You weren't doing anything important." He led Emma out of the room, giving her shoulders a gentle squeeze. "Come on, sweetheart. Brush your teeth and I'll tuck you in."

I seethed with annoyance as I went into the family room. Nothing I did was important to him. But then I thought, Stephen may be forgetful and disorganized, but he loves the kids, in his own way.

Ethan was sprawled on the floor in the family room, headphones covering his ears. Shaking my head and despairing of the men in my family, I ushered him to his room. I flopped down on the couch and put my feet up on the coffee table, a little annoyed that Stephen had hurt Emma's feelings again. Then I felt angry with myself for not demanding that he shape up and keep his promises.

The weekend flew by as it always does. I cleaned the house and prepared meals, but my thoughts kept returning to James and how, when we talked, I felt more like a fascinating, intelligent woman than a somewhat faded wife and mother. Why don't Stephen and I just sit and talk? I wondered. We used to in the early days. And then I remembered that it was Stephen who did all of the talking—about his plans, his ideas.

I waited until late Sunday afternoon for Stephen to replace the light bulb in the hallway and when he didn't, I dragged the rickety stepladder from the garage and changed it myself.

That night, Stephen struggled out of his recliner, switched off the TV, and yawned. "I'm beat. Coming to bed?" he asked.

"Later. I just want to finish this article."

"Hey, we have light," he joked, opening the door to the back hallway. He turned back to me. "Why didn't you remind me?"

"I did. Several times."

"I don't remember. Anyway, I would've gotten around to it."

"Yeah. Right."

"What's that supposed to mean?"

I looked up from my magazine. As calmly as I could, I said, "It means that someone had to do it before Ethan or Emma fell down the stairs in the dark. And could you please fix that stepladder? It's dangerous."

"Yeah, yeah—don't nag me, Mouse. It's on my list."

Along with a million other things, I thought angrily. And don't call me Mouse!

The following Friday I took my time getting ready for ladies' night. It was fun to dress up and I wished again that Stephen would take me somewhere nice. On the few occasions when I'd had the courage to suggest it to him, he'd complained of being tired. However, whenever Barry called and said that he was going drinking or bowling, Stephen was always out the door before you could say, "Budweiser."

I stared at my reflection in the mirror. What about me? I thought. I work full time and take care of the kids and the house, but I'd still love to go out for dinner or dancing every once in awhile. But I knew it wouldn't happen.

I applied more mascara, thinking bitterly, To hell with Stephen!

Downstairs, Stephen, Ethan, and Emma were watching a DVD. "I'll see you later," I told them.

Stephen looked up from his recliner. "Remind me again where you're going?"

"Out with Lauren."

"Oh, yeah, right." His eyes slid back to the screen.

During the drive to Bentonville, Lauren regaled me with how much fun she'd had the previous week. Troy, the Stetson guy, took her home that night and he planned to be at the club again.

"He's nice," Lauren said, shrugging, "but it's too soon to tell if he's the right man for me."

"Seems like there're plenty of fish in the sea, still, and this club is one big ocean," I remarked as we got out of the car.

"Yeah, and I'm not going to rush things." She turned to me. "You look nice tonight."

"Thanks." I knew that I did look good; I'd brushed my hair until my golden highlights shone and a new, brown eye shadow really brought out my eyes. I wore my best, sexiest, little black dress and four-inch heels, to boot.

Still, I found myself holding my breath as my eyes searched the room for James. He wasn't there and all at once I was disappointed, but I settled down to people-watch. Lauren stayed with me until Troy walked in. Then he waved her over to a table near the small stage.

That night there was live music from a local country group called The Tumbleweeds. They're pretty good, and I soon found my feet tapping to the rhythm. Several men asked me to dance, but I declined. My eyes sought my friend, dancing with Troy as I thought, I won't need to come next week. Lauren's found someone she likes and even if it doesn't work out, she'll feel confident enough to come alone from now on. I'll go back to family pizza night.

I used to look forward to those nights when the four of us would get together, especially when the kids were younger. We always ate in the family room and watched DVDs rented from Netflix. Increasingly, though, family nights were a rarity. Ethan hung out more with his friends and Emma seemed to be constantly invited to sleepovers and during the last few movies we rented, Stephen and I ate our pizza in silence and then he fell asleep, missing half the action.

"Hello."

It was James. My stomach did a complete flip, just like I was a teenager back in high school with an insane crush on the football star who was finally speaking to me.

"Hi," I said, as casually as I could, watching him lower himself onto the chair across from mine at the small table. He reached out to shake my hand; his fingers were cold and I shivered.

"Sorry; I hurried out without a jacket."

The idea: He was rushing to see me! popped into my head. Then I thought: That's nonsense. James dragged his chair closer to mine and we fell into easy conversation. He didn't even check out the other women and I felt flattered. But when he asked me to dance, I declined. Already, Stephen had inquired as to what I did there, and I told him that I just sat and talked with people, so I imagined he'd be upset if he knew I was dancing with men and I didn't want the aggravation that that might cause. My conscience was clear because I was being friendly, and nothing more.

Lauren appeared and announced that she was leaving with Troy. I glanced at my watch; it was almost midnight and I couldn't imagine where the time went. Turning away from Lauren's curious gaze, I spoke to James.

"I've gotta run."

"Pity," he replied. "I was enjoying myself."

"Me, too."

"Will you be here next week?"

134

"I'm—I'm not sure," I stammered, flustered, wanting to return and yet feeling guilty about wanting to.

"Please try," he said. "I'll be waiting for you."

When I got home, Stephen was asleep in his recliner. I had to wake him up so we could go to bed. "You could've called and told me that you'd be late," he grumbled.

The following Friday I told Stephen a lie. I told him that I was driving Lauren to Bentonville again, even though her car had been fixed and she was making her own way there.

"What? Hasn't she found a new guy yet?" Stephen whined like a child given a time-out. "And it's family night."

I paused in the action of reaching for my car keys. "Sorry; not tonight. Don't tell me you've forgotten already that Ethan's at Jason's and Emma will be at the ice rink until ten." I could tell from the look on his face that he had not remembered. "Don't worry," I continued. "They both have rides so you won't need to pick them up. There's lasagna in the oven and a salad in the fridge; you have the whole evening to yourself."

"Well, I won't wait up if you're late," Stephen said, practically pouting.

Heading out the door I plucked up the courage to say, "Maybe you'll find time to put those doors back on the cabinets later, huh?"

He actually had the nerve to glare at me. "I'll be joining Barry and the guys for a few beers."

I shrugged. "Suit yourself."

At the club, I pulled into the parking lot and checked my hair in my rearview mirror. I suppose lots of people live this way, I mused, living lives that revolve around their families. But what'll Stephen and I talk about once the kids leave home? Will I still be waiting for him to finish some do-it-yourself project, afraid to speak my mind?

The very idea made me shudder.

James strolled up to my car and held the door open for me. "Hey, beautiful," he drawled. "You look terrific."

My lips formed a wide smile. "Thanks." The weather had improved drastically over the last few days—a typical north Texas winter spike. I was wearing a blue peasant blouse and a short, denim skirt with vintage cowboy boots and I felt feminine, hip, sexy, fun, stylish, and desirable. James wore starched Wranglers that hugged his slim hips and at the sight, my mind flew briefly to Stephen's belly, which grows bigger every year.

Not to mention the fact that James's compliment contrasted sharply with my husband's lack of observation. As it was, Stephen was generally more concerned about being alone, and that didn't even mean that he was missing me in particular; he just liked to stick to his regular routine and treat me more like a live-in housekeeper than a wife and life partner.

But I won't think about that now, I told myself as James and I entered the club. When James asked me what I wanted to drink, I told him white wine. I wanted to do something wild that night, but drinking white wine was about as rebellious as I got.

Nonetheless, the alcohol relaxed me and I began to appreciate how nice it is, being with someone who treats you with respect and appreciation. James asked my opinions about things, laughed at my jokes, and I felt like a wholly different woman that night—a fantastic woman, in fact, in every sense of the word. And then it started to dawn on me: Away from the pressures of my home situation, I'm free to be myself.

That night I agreed to dance. James's eyebrows shot up with surprise. "At last!" he said, pulling me to my feet before I could change my mind. "You've refused me so many times that I was beginning to think you must have a wooden leg!"

I couldn't remember the last time I'd been dancing; I figure it must've been before Ethan was born. But James spun me around that dance floor; we danced until I was dizzy and he even taught me the Texas two-step. Later, he held me close during a slow song and I tingled all over when I felt his breath on my neck. Desire stirred deep within me, but I knew I couldn't let my mind—much less my very married body—go there. Deciding I'd better put some space between us before I did anything stupid, I finally excused myself and went to the ladies' room.

"Hurry back," James called after me.

In the ladies' room, I held my wrists under the tap to refresh myself with the cold, running water. How can this stranger have such an effect on me? I wondered. But James is no stranger; I know him pretty well now. In fact, we're friends now and I can't bear the thought of never seeing him again.

"Meadow?" It was Lauren. "What are you doing in here?"

All at once guilt and panic gripped me as I thought, She knows about my secret crush on James. She'll tell Stephen! I switched off the faucet and grabbed a paper towel from the dispenser. "Oh, hi, Lauren," I said, drying my hands to give myself time to think. "I just needed to get out of the house for a while—you know how it is. Stephen's up to his ears in do-it-yourself stuff and I enjoyed being here these last few Fridays; I guess I'm not quite as ready to stop coming as I thought I was."

Her features relaxed; she found her lipstick and faced the

mirror and then she snorted. "And to think—I'm here craving a quiet night at home!" She stepped back to admire her reflection. "Don't you and Stephen ever go out together anymore?"

I shook my head. "We haven't in a long time. But that could change now that the kids are getting older. Maybe I'll persuade him to take me dancing."

Lauren smiled and went on her way. Relief washed over me as I realized that I'd managed to lie my way out of the situation, but being reminded again that Stephen never took me anywhere made me more resolved than ever to continue to see James.

If he wants that, I anxiously amended.

When I returned to our table James held my chair for me as I sat and all at once, the contrast between him and my husband seemed even more pronounced. Stephen never treated me like a lady and his constant use of my nickname, "Mouse," which he gave me back in our early years together as a sort of gentle, affectionate teasing, was now hateful to me.

I caught James's eye and blurted out, "I can't come here anymore."

He studied my face carefully, his beautiful eyes instantly filled with genuine concern. "Is your husband putting his foot down? I'm not surprised. I wouldn't let you out of my sight if you were my wife."

Oh, what a nice thing to say, I thought, practically glowing all over. But I said, "My friend's found someone nice."

James draped one muscular arm across the back of my chair. "I understand, but I sure wish I could keep on seeing you; I really like you, you know. Isn't there any way. . .?"

My heart started pounding faster than it did during the two-step. "I like you, too," I said, blushing furiously. "Maybe . . . well, I have a yoga class on Tuesday nights, but—"

"Where?"

"At the Y."

"How about you give that a miss and meet me at Ruffalo's on the town square?"

I lowered my eyes from his intense gaze. "Okay."

James and I started to meet regularly.

At first I was scared that someone I knew might see us together, but there was never anyone I knew in Ruffalo's. I tried to convince myself that men and women can have perfectly harmless, platonic relationships—that they don't always have to lead to sex—but whenever James walked toward me my heart started pounding and his crooked, easy grin and blue eyes always took my breath away.

I awoke one Saturday knowing that I didn't have to dive out of bed; I could take my time. Stephen's side of the bed was empty, I noticed. Stretching like a cat, I let my mind drift to James, wondering in a kind of contentedly wondrous daze, What's come over me? Is being treated kindly something I crave so much that I have to get that need met by someone—even if that someone is someone other than my husband?

Yes, it's true, I finally admitted to myself. Stephen doesn't meet my needs for romance or excitement. He may be a good provider and a good father, but he definitely lacks something as a husband.

The idea that part of the problem might be my inability to speak up for myself and my unwillingness to risk confrontation, I brushed aside. James and I are friends and nothing more, I decided, and so my conscience was clear, although my body decried the fact. I longed for his touch, but he, gentleman that he is, neither said nor did anything that caused me to feel bad about meeting him.

In fact, I can still remember the time I asked him, "Are you still hoping to find Miss Right?"

His eyes held mine and they darkened as if the sun had gone behind a cloud. "I've already found her," he whispered. "Only, she belongs to someone else."

That's when I realized that I was right all along—James and I felt the same way about each other, but our timing was way off. All of a sudden my imagination hurtled out of control for a moment as I fervently wished that I were single again. But just as quickly, I brought myself back to reality with one abiding thought: I love Ethan and Emma and I would never do anything to hurt them. And so I pulled down the shutters over "what if."

"I'm sure you'll find someone," I told James briskly.

Back in the present, loud banging broke my train of thought. Scrambling into my robe I hurried downstairs to find Stephen standing in the middle of our family room. Strips of paneling littered the floor around him and even as I gingerly stepped over a pile of rubble, he ripped another piece off the wall. Dust and powdered sheetrock filled the air.

"Just what, exactly, are you doing?" I demanded, hands on my hips.

He turned to face me. "Oh, hi, Mouse. I thought I'd make a start in here, but wouldn't you know it? The guy who installed this used glue and it's harder to—"

"For heaven's sake!" I fumed. "The stairs aren't even painted yet and the kitchen's a mess and you promised you'd finish that before you did anything else!"

138

Stephen blinked behind his protective glasses. "I can do that some other time."

I trembled with fury as tears sprang to my eyes. "This is too much! I'm fed up with your procrastination! Why can't you finish one thing before you start another?"

"But—"

"Don't 'but' me! Honestly, Stephen! You drive me crazy! We're living in a building site! In fact, I've been living in one for ten years now! How can I possibly keep the house nice and clean when you're forever tearing it apart?"

My outburst seemed to surprise him. He sat back on his heels. "It's never bothered you before."

"Yes, it has, but I've let it slide and I can't go through this again! You won't even let me help you so it's done quicker!"

"Meadow. . . ." He removed the glasses and the scornful look in his eyes said it all: You're weak, Meadow. You're a mouse.

And that's when I realized: I am a mouse. I squeak about things under my breath, but I never come right out and say them.

Immediately, I regretted my outburst. "Yeah, I know. I can't do the heavy work, and I don't paint as well as you do . . . but you could show me."

"Aren't things perfect when I've finished?" he snapped.

As usual, I backed down before he could accuse me of being like Mom. "Yes, eventually," I agreed, swallowing the hard, painful lump in my throat. "But there's so much left unfinished . . . and half the time you're out with your buddies and. . . ."

It was a futile argument and I knew it. Stephen does just as he pleases and I let him, I realized. He'll continue to switch from project to project, constantly leaving stuff lying around, forgetting to pick up the kids and going out whenever he wants.

I dug my fingernails into my palms to keep myself from screaming. "I give up, Stephen. I'm going to make coffee."

"Would you bring me a cup while you're at it?"

My words didn't make one scrap of difference, I thought. "Whatever," I said.

The kids were upset about the family room suddenly being "out-of-bounds."

"It's not my fault," I told them tersely.

"But I wanna watch that DVD Lindsay lent me!" Emma whined.

"You could've asked Dad to wait until school's out." Ethan pouted. "I have a report to finish for Monday."

I honestly felt like asking them—my own kids—Since when has your father ever listened to me?

They moped about until I finally sent them to their friends' homes to use their computers and TVs. Then I started to make a grocery list, but I couldn't concentrate with Stephen ripping walls apart.

I got into the car. Instead of heading to the supermarket, though, I drove to the park. After jogging twice round the lake to try and rid myself of some pent-up emotion, I sat on a bench and watched the ducks. They floated past me on the smooth water like they didn't have a care in the world and I found myself thinking, I wish my life were that simple.

Then all at once I thought, I have to talk to someone before I explode! Lauren sprang to mind, but I knew she was just getting her life back on track. The only other person I could think of was James. He'll listen to me, I decided. After all, he knows all about my problems with Stephen.

I dialed James's number on my cell. The pleasure I heard in his voice when he realized it was I made me glad I called. And after just a few words he instinctively sensed that I was upset.

"Where are you?" he asked.

"In the park."

"Want me to come there?"

Instantly, I felt my spirits lift to the heavens. "Would you?"

Ten minutes later we sat on that bench and talked. Though he asked me what was troubling me, I wouldn't elaborate. "Just stuff," I said. "You don't want to hear it." Suddenly, now that James was there, I didn't want to talk about Stephen at all.

James reached for my hand then and as our fingers touched, I grasped hold of him like I was drowning. He pulled me close and the warmth of his chest seeped into my weary body.

"I'm just so lonely and fed up," I said as hot tears trickled down my cheeks.

His thumbs gently brushed my tears away. "I'm here for you, Meadow."

Then he kissed me, gently.

James is my one-and-only comfort, I thought then. He'll never do anything to annoy or upset me.

I returned his kisses and gradually, they erased all of my frustrations. The touch of his lips on mine sent frissons of pleasure through me like rivulets; a wonderful, building heat began in my groin and spread slowly through my body until my breasts tingled and swelled. I opened my mouth and his tongue flicked against mine and a feeling of pure bliss enveloped me.

After awhile he pulled back and gazed deeply into my eyes. "Are you sure about this?" he asked in a husky, gentle whisper.

It was the first time a man ever asked me what I wanted.

140

"Yes. Don't stop. I want you to kiss me. I want you to . . . I want . . . you."

I followed him to his place, where we made love. I felt vibrant, and alive—a totally different woman.

After that day, instead of meeting at Ruffalo's I'd park my car outside the Y where James would be waiting on his Harley. Riding behind him, my arms wrapped around his waist, I felt like a princess being whisked away from her prison tower by a leather-clad knight. For a few precious hours all my problems miraculously disappeared.

Back home, I tackled the demands of my family with renewed energy. I finally didn't care whether or not Stephen finished his jobs; I encouraged him to meet up with his friends and while he was out I took long, relaxing bubble baths and pampered myself. I helped Ethan with his schoolwork and talked Emma through her first real argument with her best friend. Nonetheless, it took lots of concentration to juggle all of the balls—work, home, family, and James—so that no one discovered my secret. I wondered why I wasn't consumed with guilt and decided that there was nothing to feel guilty about; James supplied my need for romance. No one was suffering; I took very good care of my family.

Stephen had no idea about how my improved outlook on life came about, but he seemed to like it nonetheless. We got along so much better because I was finally happy again, and it showed. If Stephen called me "Mouse," I'd smile indulgently and think: Little does he know that his mouse has escaped from her cage.

Time slipped by. It was a warm Saturday evening in summer and we'd just finished eating barbequed chicken, corn on the cob, and homemade potato salad. Emma and Ethan were in the kitchen doing the dishes; I'd finally decided that it was time they pulled their weight around the house; I didn't want them to end up as irresponsible as their father. It'd been a battle of wills and there were plenty of screaming matches and slammed doors, but I stuck to my resolution. Now they knew that if they didn't do their chores, they'd lose privileges. Stephen seemed bewildered by my new assertiveness with the kids, but he'd agreed to back me up.

I sipped my wine, enjoying the warm air on my "sun-kissed" arms—James's words. I'd blushed when he said that a couple of weeks ago; since then he'd been swamped with work and we hadn't seen each other. I was anxious to be with him again.

"Meadow?" Stephen's voice demanded my attention.

"Hmm?"

"I was talking about our vacation."

"Vacation?"

141

"Snap out of it, Mouse. We have to plan our trip to Oklahoma. I've chosen a campsite; it's in—"

"I'm not going."

"What?" Stephen's mouth hung open. "You don't want to come?"

"No. Why don't you take Ethan and Emma? They'd love some one-on-one time with you. You could teach them to fish."

"Fish?" Stephen's eyebrows shot up to his hairline. "I've never fished in my life. How—?"

"Oh. Well, then maybe you could learn, too."

"But—"

"No, really, Stephen—it's a great idea."

"And what will you do?"

I smiled. "I'll sleep late and eat out instead of having to cook every night. I'll have a massage at the day spa and read books."

But I knew how I really wanted to spend my time, and the more I thought about it the better it sounded. James always wanted me to stay longer and I always told him it was impossible, but here was our chance. We could try out recipes in his neat, modern kitchen, make love whenever we felt like it, and relax for hours in his luxurious hot tub. As it was, my whole body flushed with anticipation whenever I thought about it—finally, our opportunity to have some quality time together instead of just scant stolen moments.

"Meadow!"

I picked up my glass. "I'm going to see how the kids are doing."

A few days later, lying in James's arms, I told him about my plan.

"Really?" he said. "You'll be able to spend the whole week with me?"

"Yes. Won't it be wonderful?"

He nuzzled my neck. "Perfect. It'll be like we're a real couple."

I checked the time, not quite hearing his words. "I have to get dressed."

James grabbed my arm as I swung my legs off the bed. "It's still early."

"No, it's late."

He kissed my fingers and then reluctantly released me. "Okay. I'll let you go this time, but at least you're finally ready to take our relationship further."

Halfway to the bathroom, I stopped. I turned back to face him. "What do you mean?"

"You're getting ready to leave Stephen, aren't you?"

"What?"

I'd been living my fantasy: family, job, and lover. Why would I want that to change? I suddenly realized. Time spent with James had always been too short, too precious to waste any of it really talking; I never thought further ahead than our next rendezvous.

James's eyes were accusing. "I want a permanent relationship, Meadow. I want children—yours, of course, and maybe one of our own, too. Don't you want that, too?"

His words whirled around in my head. James is right, I thought suddenly. This can't go on forever. Relationships evolve. They grow and mature. But am I honestly ready to leave behind everything I've ever known for something new? Once, I loved Stephen deeply; I just hate the way we behave toward each other nowadays. Now, though, I have some serious thinking to do.

I opened the bathroom door. "Let's discuss it next time," I told James.

During the drive home I came to the conclusion that I had to end my relationship with James and try to make things right with Stephen. I realized I'd made a bad call, searching outside my marriage for companionship, but since then I felt I'd changed—a lot. I figured if I could finally stand up for myself, once and for all, things would be better.

I'll miss James terribly, I mused as I drove along, but there's no real substance to our relationship, no history of problem solving. He just enjoys being in love and I honestly get the feeling that if it weren't me, he'd find someone else to care for and pamper. I can't hold him back from finding a woman who can give him everything he wants when I can't really give him anything at all.

I shed a few tears, but finally convinced myself I was right as I turned into our driveway.

Before I reached the house, Stephen yanked open the front door and stormed out onto the porch. "Where the hell have you been?" he demanded. Frown lines creased his forehead.

"What's the matter?"

"It's Ethan."

My footsteps quickened as I rushed past Stephen and into the house. "What's wrong with him?"

Inside, Ethan lay on the couch in the family room, his left arm in a sling, a bandage across one cheekbone.

"Ethan!" I cried. "What happened?"

"Sorry, Mom. I was only trying to get the ball."

Stephen explained. "Ethan was tossing his baseball around the yard. It got stuck in the gutter and he climbed the stepladder and—"

"And he fell off?" I finished. My eyes flashed fire at Stephen.

143

"How many times have I asked you to fix that stupid stepladder? I knew something like this would happen!" I knelt down and gently explored the bruises on Ethan's forehead with my fingertips. He pushed me away.

"I'm okay, Mom. It's no big deal."

Stephen pulled on my arm. "Come into the kitchen, please."

After the door closed, I let fly. "How dare you let our son get hurt because you're too preoccupied to—"

He held up a hand to silence me. "Where were you tonight?" His voice was serious, his lips a grim, tight line.

"At yoga, of course. Where's Emma?"

"Spending the night at Lindsay's; I couldn't cope with her, too. Listen to me, Meadow—it's your job to care for the kids when they're sick, not mine. I'd planned to meet Barry, but I ended up spending the evening at the hospital in the—"

"What do you mean, it's my job?"

He ignored my question. "Why didn't you check your messages?"

Because I was too preoccupied with thinking about breaking up with James. "I, um. . . ."

Stephen grabbed my shoulders. "Look at me, Meadow."

I found it hard to meet his eyes. I was in another man's arms when my son was hurt, I realized. I felt sick.

"Ethan will be fine," Stephen said. "He has a sprained wrist and some bruising, that's all. I kept calling your cell and then I finally tried the Y. They told me you weren't in any class and after I told them that it was an emergency, they checked and told me that your car wasn't even parked in their lot."

I sagged against the counter, feeling as fragile as glass.

"I told Ethan you probably went for coffee with Lauren. Did you?"

It sounded to me like Stephen suspected something, but wasn't entirely sure. All I have to do, I realized, is tell him that I went for coffee and everything will return to normal. But disgust with my own actions mutated into anger toward Stephen. As a father, I thought furiously, he should put his kids before his drinking buddies. And he never fixed that stepladder, even after I asked him countless times. This is his fault as much as mine.

The words left my lips before I could stop them. "I wasn't with Lauren."

Stephen stared at me. "Then where were you?"

"I was with . . . someone else."

"You mean . . . another man?"

"Yes." What am I doing? I wondered incredulously. I must be

144

crazy! I can't believe I'm confessing to my affair, especially when I've already decided that it's over. I held my breath.

Stephen's eyes swept over me like he was seeing me for the very first time. "You're joking, right? You? Give me a break. You're nothing but a—"

"A mouse?" Anger surged through me. Stephen never took anything I said seriously. I lifted my chin, thinking, I won't back down anymore. I've gone this far. . . . "Well, this mouse has teeth, as well as feelings, and needs! I'm not an animal, Stephen. I'm a human being—a woman—and I deserve to be treated like one!"

His arms dropped to his sides and he took a step back, surprised by my forcefulness. As his eyes searched mine, the meaning of my words continued to sink in. "Who is it?"

"His name is James."

"Where did you meet? How long have you been seeing him?"

"We met at a club. The one I've been going to with Lauren."

"I should've known something was going on. You've been too nice lately." The tendons in his neck bulged and his eyes narrowed. "How dare you do this to me, Meadow?"

"You only think of yourself, don't you?" I hissed.

Stephen's lip curled. "It's all about sex, isn't it? I don't get it; you never seemed to care for it that much."

I lowered my voice. "Really? Well, it's no fun when it's just one more duty I'm expected to perform. But you're wrong, anyway; it isn't just about the sex. James makes me feel special. He treats me like a princess and he—"

Stephen glared at me with fury in his eyes. His hands bunched into fists. He brought them down and punched the countertop and I flinched and cried out as dishes rattled and silverware clattered to the floor.

"Mom?" Ethan called out from the family room. "What's going on?"

Quickly, I poked my head around the door. "It's okay, honey; I just dropped something. Do you want a soda?"

"Yeah."

I turned back to Stephen. He was pacing the floor, cursing under his breath.

"We can't discuss this now," I told him, taking a Coke from the refrigerator.

Stephen ripped the can out of my hand and threw it against the wall. Then he shoved his face into mine. "You're right," he spat. "There's nothing to talk about. I'm packing my bags!"

"Bags?" My temples throbbed, but I tried to stay calm. "You can't leave when Ethan—"

He whirled around. "How can I stay, knowing you've been cheating on me?"

I put my head in my hands. I don't know what I thought he'd say. Maybe I wanted him to plead with me to give up James, or tell me that he loved me, or ask me how he could change to make me happy again. Instead, he was giving up without a fight.

Looking up, I said, "You've cheated on me, too, giving your time to your buddies or the TV."

Stephen said not a word.

"Okay; be a coward," I continued. "Run away. I don't need you any more."

My words were strangely empowering. Stephen walked away, shoulders slumped, the back of his neck an angry red. I realized I'd taken a huge risk in telling the truth and standing up to him; I couldn't believe that he didn't know how to deal with me when I did that.

But when has he ever really dealt with problems? I realized.

I cleaned up the soda spill while the hammering of my heart lessened, got another Coke from the fridge, and carried it out to Ethan.

At first I felt numb, but soon the feeling of relief that came from finally speaking up for myself made me strong. Yes, it's true—my worst nightmare came true: Stephen left me. I didn't realize until it happened how much I'd feared that! But when it finally happened, I didn't fall apart.

That's when I realized that I could—and would—manage.

Sounding more confident than I felt, I told the children the next day that their father and I were going through "a rough time." But they were "not to worry," we would "sort things out."

"Daddy and I love you," I told them, "we'll always love you, and you two are in no way to blame for any of this."

When I drove over to James's house on Sunday, I found him in his garage, cleaning his bike.

"Stephen knows about us," I told him, standing on the driveway. "He's moved out."

James looked up from polishing the chrome of the Harley. He grinned widely like he just found out he won some sort of contest. "So? When are you moving in with me?"

"I'm—I'm not."

"What? But you're free now."

"James," I said as he hurried toward me, "I care for you, but . . . but there's a lot more to love. I've realized—perhaps too late—that problem solving is part of love and I need to do that . . . with Stephen. I'm really sorry. You've been absolutely wonderful

146

to me and you've really allowed me to be myself. I want to thank you for that from the bottom of my heart."

James threw his arms around me. "No, no—don't say that. You can't—"

I pulled away; his embrace was too inviting and I felt safe there, but I'd already made up my mind. Even if it didn't work out between Stephen and me, I wouldn't go back to James on the same terms as before. "Please, let me finish," I said.

"I don't understand." He drew away and leaned against the wall looking sad and confused.

I took a deep breath. "James, I'd already planned to end our relationship before Stephen found out. You deserve someone who wants more than an affair."

"Meadow, please. I love you," James pleaded, his voice gritty with emotion. "You'll change your mind . . . I can wait."

I shook my head and hurried from the yard. The sooner I leave him, I thought, the quicker he can heal.

Back at home I sobbed for an hour and then dried my tears. I knew I did the right thing with James, but the weight of my earlier poor judgment began to take its toll. I didn't sleep well and dark circles appeared under my eyes; I hated the realization that I broke up my family unit.

Stephen slept on Barry's floor for a few days and then found a hotel room. He contacted a lawyer and refused to talk to me about anything other than the kids. He blustered and acted like I was the only one to blame for the split. I said nothing.

The kids needed something to do during school vacation so they wouldn't have time to worry about Stephen and me, so during my week off I got books and videos on do-it-yourself from the library. They reluctantly agreed to help me complete some of the unfinished projects; I figured if we had to sell the house, we'd get a better price if it didn't look like a work in progress.

Honestly, it was all trial and error, but the renovating and decorating turned out to be therapeutic for all of us. Soon, Ethan's baseboards gleamed with a fresh coat of paint; the family room had fresh drywall one weekend and it was painted the next. Emma and Ethan laughed like toddlers, splashing paint on each other, but they glowed with satisfaction when I praised them for their hard work.

Then one Friday, Stephen called to collect the children for the weekend. Normally he waited outside in the car but on that day he handed me a bunch of papers to read. I invited him in and he stood silently in the family room, ignoring me, while Ethan and Emma fetched their bags. I watched as Stephen looked around the room. His eyes took in the freshly painted walls, the built-in bookcases, and the new valance over the window.

"Watch this, Daddy!" Emma came through the door and turned the dimmer switch. The lights went low. "Isn't this great for watching TV?"

"Who did all this?" Stephen asked.

My chest swelled with pride. "The three of us," I told him, and Emma nodded to convince Stephen that I was telling the truth.

Ethan joined us. "Hey, Dad. Didn't we do a great job?"

"Sure, Ethan . . . sure. The room looks . . . terrific."

My eyes sought Stephen's. There was a look of despondency in them. "Seems I'm not needed around here, after all," he said quietly.

"Nonsense," I quickly replied. "We haven't done half as good a job as you'd have done, but it doesn't have to be perfect, does it?"

"I suppose not," he said, clenching his jaw like it was painful for him to admit it. "But it's good enough."

"That's all I want." All I ever wanted, I thought, watching Stephen stand there like a lost child. I never asked for absolute perfection. On impulse, I suggested, "Why don't you stay for dinner on Sunday after you bring Ethan and Em back? You could help me hang Em's doors. I haven't figured out how to do that and get them level."

His face brightened like I'd just handed him a lifeline. "Okay. Sounds good."

I held the papers he gave me to my chest. "Then we can discuss our future."

That weekend as I roamed around the empty house, smiling family photos on our mantelpiece mocked me. Our wedding portrait reminded me of my broken vows and I thought about what sort of role model I was for my kids. I went about things entirely the wrong way, I realized. But if I start making amends now, maybe it won't be too late for them. I must teach Em to have self-worth, and to speak up for herself—to always know that she can always ask for what she wants in life.

And Ethan? He needs to learn that women are men's equals, and that he should always listen so that he can treat people fairly and not walk all over them.

As I baked an apple pie I came to the understanding that my future behavior had to be in the best interests of my children. As it was, they were casualties of a war not of their making. I knew that I'd made a mistake and that there was no turning back, but I also finally understood that I had to take care of myself so that I would have the strength to deal with life.

I ran a few errands Sunday afternoon and when I returned I spotted Stephen's car parked at the curb in front of our house. As I hurried up the driveway, I caught a glimpse of Stephen, Ethan, and Emma inside the house, all seated around the kitchen table. I stopped in my tracks, watching them. The children laughed at something Stephen said and Em reached over and tapped him playfully on the arm. Stephen's face was beaming like it used to when the kids were small.

Suddenly, watching them, everything was crystal clear: This is where I want to be—part of a loving, happy family unit. That's my validation. And I can have that with Stephen instead of running around looking for it from someone else. I'll make him realize how sorry I am, if he'll only listen to me.

I took a deep breath and opened the door. "Sorry I'm late," I called out.

"We're in here, Mom," Ethan called back, "playing Uno."

"Can I join in?" I asked as I strode into the kitchen.

The children looked warily at Stephen. "Sure," he said, and I saw Ethan and Emma glance at each other with relief.

Later, I cooked steaks and baked potatoes. Stephen wolfed down the apple pie I presented for dessert, making me wonder if he'd been eating enough. He's already visibly thinner, I realized.

After we all helped fit Em's closet doors, she and Ethan went to their rooms leaving Stephen and me alone. I took the papers (they were a request for a legal separation) into the family room. Stephen carried his beer through and set a glass of wine for me on the coffee table.

"We had fun tonight, didn't we?" Stephen remarked from his recliner.

"Yes. Just like old times." Strange, but I got a thrill of pleasure, seeing my husband sitting in his usual place. But this isn't the old Stephen, I realized. He seems more serious, thoughtful.

Stephen waved a hand to indicate the kids upstairs. "They're growing up fast."

"Yes. It's hard to believe that Ethan will be thirteen next month."

"I guess he's old enough to take care of Em if we go out together some night." He paused. "Will you have dinner with me, Mead?"

I hid my surprise by gulping down my wine, hoping I wouldn't choke on it. Finally, I cleared my throat and managed, "I'd like that."

"Okay, then."

I didn't know what to make of his invitation. Is he asking

me on a date? I wondered. I decided to make no excuses for my actions and go along with whatever he wanted to do, just as long as we had joint guardianship of the children. That was one thing I knew I would never relinquish.

I handed Stephen the papers. "I've signed these," I told him.

"Oh. Well, it's only a temporary thing." He dropped them onto the floor beside his recliner.

"Is it?"

"Yeah. We don't have to take it any further."

"I was under the impression that you want a divorce."

"Yes—I mean—no. I did, but. . . ." He raked his fingers through his hair. "I've been thinking about marriage counseling."

"Marriage counseling?"

"Yes. Are you still seeing that guy?" he asked, watching me closely for my reaction to the question.

I shook my head. "No. I ended it."

"When?"

"I'd already decided to end it the night Ethan got hurt. If it hadn't been for that and me finally speaking out, you might never have known."

"Why didn't you tell me?"

"I didn't think you'd believe me."

Stephen looked down at his feet. "Were you . . . careful?" he asked.

"Very."

"Are you sorry it's over?"

"Not at all, but I've learned from it."

My words lingered, like snowflakes frozen in midair. Stephen drained his beer.

"Would you like another?" I asked.

"No, thanks. I'm cutting back."

I nodded. "I'm glad you're taking care of yourself."

He managed a small, rueful smile. "Yeah, but it's hard work."

I smiled. "Tell me about it."

He got up and paced the room like he could think better on his feet. "What did I do wrong?" he asked.

All at once my heart went out to him for his willingness to take the blame. "Stephen," I answered, "it wasn't just you. We've both been lacking. I've been too scared to tell you my real feelings all these years, so I haven't been my true self. I hope you can forgive me for that."

He stopped pacing and studied my face intently.

"I love you, and Ethan, and Emma," I continued, "and I would've liked to have had some input in this family. I don't want to be disconnected anymore, or feel invisible. Can you understand that, Stephen? Even if it means losing you for good, I must tell you how I feel. I have to do exactly that from now on or I'll lose myself for good." And then, without blaming him, I detailed my grievances.

When I'd said my piece, Stephen was silent for several minutes. Then: "You never really told me any of this before—or at least not clearly enough that I understood."

I sighed. "I couldn't speak my mind. I didn't want to nag you, like Mom did with Dad."

"You've never got over your father leaving, have you? But I wish you'd said something, sooner."

I sighed again, feeling miserable. "I thought you'd leave if I constantly nagged. Please know that I never set out to hurt our marriage."

Stephen returned to his chair. "I'm partly to blame for that, Meadow. I didn't recognize your abilities like I should have. But being alone in that hotel room has made me realize how much you do for this family."

"Things won't be the same around here if we do get back together," I told him plainly, but also as kindly as I could. "Are you prepared for that?"

He smiled and finally nodded. "Yes. I guess I am. But I know I've still got a lot to figure out."

"Then let's try counseling. I'll do whatever is asked of me."

Minutes passed, but the silence was friendly, like we were both trying to assess these "new people" in front of us. "You look different," I told him.

His lips twitched in a half-smile. "So you finally noticed, huh? I've been working out during my lunch hours and using the hotel's fitness center."

"A-ha."

"I've lost ten pounds," he boasted. "All by lifting weights and running on the treadmill."

"You look really good."

He grinned at the compliment. I sipped my wine and felt grateful that Stephen might give me a second chance. He's basically a good person, I thought. And so am I. But I didn't know how to ask for what I need without nagging. Now, though, I'm finally learning. All I want is for him to show me some affection, take me out once in a blue moon, and be romantic occasionally. Be romantic. Huh! I've been totally wrong about romance!

I used to think a man was romantic if he showered me with compliments or brought me flowers and fancy gifts. Now I know that true romance—true love, even—is doing your best for your family day in and day out, from taking out the trash to fixing meals, caring for them when they're sick, and making memories on vacations. The rest simply follows.

Stephen settled back in his recliner. "I don't want a divorce, Meadow."

I almost laughed with relief. "Neither do I."

"Good." His shoulders relaxed. "Now that I've experienced a little, bitter taste of what life would be like without you, Meadow, I . . . I took a good, long look at myself. I realize now that I'm disorganized, I'm inconsiderate, and, looking back—I guess I kinda took you for granted."

I swallowed the lump in my throat; Stephen was reaching out to me and a glimmer of hope unfurled inside of me like a newly hatched butterfly stretching its brand-new, beautiful wings.

"Thank you for saying that, Stephen."

His eyes lit up. "I'll arrange for counseling."

"Thanks."

As if suddenly afraid of revealing too much emotion, Stephen found the newspaper on the coffee table and shook it open. The ease and familiarity of that action was like a blessing somehow. "I'll pick you up on Wednesday and give you the details then, okay?" he said.

I smiled and wiped a tear from my cheek. "Sounds good to me."

Currently, Stephen and I are working with a trained marriage counselor. We're discovering things about ourselves that we'd both locked away inside of our hearts and minds years ago, but finally revealing the truth is powerfully freeing. We both understand now that once we can be completely honest with each other, we might have the chance of a whole, new, happily married life together.

In the meantime, we date two or three times a week and spend the weekends with Ethan and Em, riding our bikes in the park, having picnics, or watching movies.

We've learned a very painful lesson, but I'm hopeful that Stephen and I will get back together one day for good.

THE END

www.ingramcontent.com/pod-product-compliance
Lightning Source LLC
Chambersburg PA
CBHW071344170626
46811CB00003B/978